The Rise of Jake Hennessey

by P.J. MacLayne

The Rise of Jake Hennessey
Copyright © 2023
by P.J. MacLayne

The Rise of Jake Hennessey is a work of fiction. All names, characters, events and places found in this book are either from the author's imagination or used fictitiously. Any similarity to persons live or dead, actual events, locations, or organizations is entirely coincidental and not intended by the author.

ISBN: 978-1-7349587-3-7

Published in the United States of America

Acknowledgments

As always, thanks go to **K.M.** Guth, for her cover design and other graphic assistance. I never go wrong with giving her the freedom to let her creativity loose on my covers.

And to Angela Pryce of Angela Pryce Editing, for her sharp eyes and gentle way of pointing out my errors.

To Cornelia Amiri, for her constant encouragement and helpful ideas. I can't begin to express how much I appreciate her coming along on this adventure with me.

This book is dedicated to Jen Hardy, who has been Jake's strongest supporter since the beginning. It was her faith in him that led me to write this story. Jen, I hope this gives you the ending you think Jake deserves.

And to Danny Burt, who has always supported my efforts to put words on paper and find a story to tell, and for helping me brainstorm what the future might be.

PROLOGUE

The gullwing car door swooshed upwards, then a rubber-tipped cane thunked as it hit the blacktop. She'd made it this far, but the tautness in Harmony's shoulders didn't loosen.

"You don't have to stay there," her therapist had reminded her. "Get a hotel room in Pittsburgh. You've got nothing to prove."

Except to herself. She studied the cobalt-blue Victorian house she was parked in front of. The Aldridge house— Eli's house—now her house, again—glowed purple in the red rays of the setting sun that broke through the gloom. She hadn't been here for over two years. How many ghosts would she disturb during her stay?

A warning tingle crawled up the back of her neck, but the neighborhood was quiet, with the neighbors tucked into their houses for supper. No one was watching her. Worn out from the long drive and hours fighting bad roads, her imagination was working overtime.

She counted to ten and then ten again, swiveled, and lowered both feet to the ground. That was the easy part.

She grasped the artificial-ivory handle of the cane for support and pushed herself upright.

Pain burned from her left heel to her knee and then to her hip. Her leg buckled. She grabbed the door frame and remained upright.

It never got any better. Two years of physical therapy and several operations later, the pain still had the power to take her down. Not that she'd let her doctors know. They'd hinted at the possibility of a full-length brace. Or an amputation.

As long as she put her weight on her right foot, the hard part was over. Still, she wasn't ready to tackle the front steps. Eli wasn't there to lean on. Maybe she'd change her mind and rent a room at the chain hotel by the interstate.

She adjusted her grip on the cane and took a step.

No, she'd made it this far.

Each step towards the house got easier as she worked out the kinks from the long drive. Or ride, really. The self-driving car had done most of the work. She'd gotten stuck in construction in West Virginia and the trip took several hours longer than she'd planned. The cold autumn rain didn't help, either.

She hobbled up the steps and to the front door, taking an old-fashioned metal key out of the pouch she wore on her waist. Every time Eli had suggested updating the security of the front door, she'd vetoed getting rid of the historic mechanism. Turning the key represented coming home.

The house wasn't home anymore. Harmony turned the key anyway.

Chapter 1

On his way in, Jake Hennessey slammed the back door of The Purple Onion. He planned to head for his office and his private stash of whiskey. He should go mingle with his customers, but he needed a moment to himself.

Danny—a balding, slender guy—stood behind the desk, filling his arms with paper goods from the shelves to take out front. So much for Jake's plan.

"Everything okay, Boss?" Danny asked.

Danny had worked as a bartender for The Purple Onion back when Jake was an occasional customer, and he knew a few of Jake's secrets. Including his long-time obsession with one Harmony Duprie-Hennessey, his cousin's widow.

"It gets me every time, her being like that." The physical differences were one thing—gone was the waist long hair worn in a bun, replaced by a pure white, short cut—but Jake suspected the mental changes were the real challenge.

"Did she see you?"

"She hasn't spotted me for twenty-two years, and I wasn't going to let it happen now."

"Are you going to at least let her know you're alive now that she's back in Oak Grove?"

Jake grimaced. "I haven't figured that out."

"You can't avoid her forever. Not if she's moving back." Danny headed out of the office and Jake trailed him. "Oak Grove is down to one grocery store, one bank, and one post office. You're bound to bump into her. There's no way she won't recognize you. You're older, but you can still pass for forty. If I didn't know better, I'd think you were dying your hair."

The town of Oak Grove may have shrunk, but business had picked up in the bar. Jake hadn't made many changes since he bought it from Carl. A new TV mounted above the bar, slightly better whiskey on the shelf, and no more stale beer with the kegs swapped out often. He'd replaced the chipped glasses with cheap but serviceable ones and fixed the crack in the sidewalk out front after he tripped on it one too many times.

He'd left the interior mostly the same, clean but dark and worn-out looking, wanting to keep the same customer base; the bottom of the barrel citizens of the area. Old man Jorge with one leg, who sat on the bench outside every morning, waiting for a cup of coffee and any conversation he could rope another customer into. Krunk, who came in every Wednesday night, had one beer that he nursed for an hour, and never spoke to anyone, but had a kid who was a cop and shared inside info with Jake. Eddie, who worked at the convenience store two blocks away, did side jobs for Jake to earn extra money, and had been one of his rescues. The bar was their safe place. Jake found it useful for other reasons.

The business didn't make much money, but it offered other benefits. Like laundering the profits for the occasional jewel theft Jake indulged in. He didn't need the money from those, the bar in Cleveland provided him with a good living. It was an ego thing.

Sure, the rare, unfamiliar face would wander in, like the guy sitting by the front door. If he was an undercover cop, he was good—too good for Oak Grove's small police department. He had Fed written all over him.

Jake stuffed the paper towels on the shelves under the bar and poured himself a beer while Danny put the other supplies away. Then he wandered around the bar, gathering empty beer mugs and chatting with the regulars.

"How's it going?" he asked Viper. With a subtle jerk of his chin, he indicated the man up front.

Viper shook his head. Once. "Did you hear they might close the high school next year? Send the remaining kids down the road to the new school. That'll be a sad day for this town."

"Another nail in the coffin." Jake nodded and walked back to the bar with his hands full. As he put the dirty glasses in the tub of soapy water, he studied the stranger in the mirror. The man lifted his mug and saluted Jake before emptying it.

A surge of anticipation beat in Jake's veins. He hadn't scored a jewelry heist for a year, and the Fed held the promise of breaking the boredom. He poured a second beer, walked over, and set it in front of the man. "My office?"

The man nodded. "Took you long enough." He picked up the beer. "Lead the way."

Jake offered the stranger one of the wooden chairs, but perched himself on the edge of his desk. That left the man looking up at him, giving Jake a psychological advantage. "What's your story?"

"No niceties, no names?" The man arched his eyebrows.

"I figure you know my name. What I'm interested in is what agency you're with."

"One you've never heard of. It's a minor branch of a minor branch dealing with security. We provide bodyguard services."

"And if Angel still hates bodyguards, she isn't aware you and your people are in town."

"Angel?"

"Harmony. Mrs. Duprie-Hennessey. That's why you're here, right?"

"How you concluded that with absolutely no information…. Yes, that's why I'm here. And it's just me. Special Agent Doan Houck, FASS. Federal Agency for Security Services." He reached into his pocket and tossed a business card on the desk.

Jake didn't like the direction the conversation was headed. He stood, walked around to the back of the desk, and settled into his comfortable office chair. "What does any of this have to do with me?"

"I don't want to bore you with politics. We're a small, under-funded agency. We rely on information other agencies share with us." Houck scratched the back of his neck. "Oak Grove isn't under the eye of any federal investigation, and no one has any intelligence to give us. We're starting from scratch. We're working with the police department, of course, but I hoped that because of your past association with the Hennesseys, you'd be willing to help procure informants."

He put his beer on Jake's desk and crossed his arms. "It appears you have the right connections."

Not ones that Jake would share. He twirled a finger in the air. "The Oak Grove rumor mill is alive and well. What are you protecting her from?"

Houck shook his head. "That's classified."

Jake opened the bottom drawer of his desk, took out his special whiskey, and poured himself a shot, pointedly not offering any to the agent. He took a sip and let the liquid lay on his tongue, savoring the hint of smoke and caramel before swallowing it.

"Let's lay this on the line," Jake said. "I don't trust you. The accident was two years ago. Harmony's been in no shape to work for any federal agency since then. It's only been in the past six months that she's taken full charge of Shifter Technologies, the company that her late husband started. Are you trying to make me believe in that time, all the federal agencies combined couldn't eliminate the threats to her?"

"You know too much for someone who's been out of touch for twenty-two years." The wooden chair scraped across the floor as Houck stood, placing both hands on the desk and leaning in so his face was inches from Jake's.

"Sit your ass back in that chair, Agent," Jake said,

his voice as icy as wind-driven hail. "If you're going to protect Harmony, you're going to have to deal with me. I don't expect you to trust me, but you'll need to follow my rules."

Houck's hot breath blew on Jake's face. "You're fooling yourself if you think you can protect her better than the U.S. government."

"The U.S. government didn't do such a good job two years ago when Eli was killed in the same wreck that left Harmony crippled for life."

"We lost one of ours in that incident." Houck sank into the wooden chair. "He and I went to The Academy together. The official report listed it as accidental, but many of us didn't believe it."

Jake took a glass off the shelf behind him, poured a shot of whiskey, and pushed it across the desk towards Houck. Houck picked it up and raised it in a salute, which Jake matched.

"So, what are the chances that the current threat against Harmony is tied to the crash?" Jake eventually asked.

"There's no specific intelligence. All we have are vague rumors. Our best guess is that it's tied to the project she and Mr. Hennessey were working on—an analysis of communications from an underground rebel movement of one of our overseas allies. I can't be more specific than that."

"And you think agents of this faction are still after Harmony?"

"That's our best take on the limited information we have. With the additional people coming to town for your former police chief's funeral, the agency doesn't want to take any chances."

Jake snorted. "The only way to protect Harmony during Chief Sorenson's funeral is to talk her out of going. That won't happen. He was a father figure."

"Don't you have any influence on her?"

"Twenty-two years ago, representatives of the FBI, ATF, DCSA, and a Florida law-enforcement agency pulled me aside and strongly encouraged me to cut ties with Eli and Harmony. I honored their requests." Mostly. He and Eli had kept in contact, but Houck didn't need to know that. "As far as Harmony is concerned, I dropped off the face of the earth after she and Eli got married."

Even when she was in the hospital, he hadn't gone to visit. Not that he hadn't tried. There'd been too much security for him to get past. He'd ended up calling in favors and relying on other people to keep him updated on her condition. Several months after the crash, when she'd recovered enough to arrange it and Eli's memorial service had finally been held, Jake had attended in disguise.

"I'm aware of your history. For Mrs. Duprie-Hennessey's safety, you need to continue your *persona non grata* status. I'll request additional personnel," Houck said.

Jake would make his own decision about staying hidden or not. "The funeral is in two days. You don't have time. You might be able to get FBI agents out of

Pittsburgh, but that's about it. Our best bet would be to have Detective Thomason babysit her, but he's probably busy with arrangements for the funeral."

"What options do I have?" Houck rotated his glass on the desktop.

"You stick to her like glue. Prepare for more than a few sleepless nights. Luckily, the house has top-notch security. Get in touch with a guy named Lando at her company. I think he's the CEO now, so you might need to use your official status to get through to him. Ask him for access to the system and tell him it's so you can protect Harmony. He'll do anything for her. You'll be able to get real-time reports on that fancy watch of yours."

Out of habit, Jake had already sized up the watch and determined the black market price. It wasn't worth the effort needed to steal it as it wasn't top of the line. It was a government-issued model from two years ago, and the arm display pixelated about half the time. Besides, Jake owned a better one that had been hacked and made untraceable.

Houck tapped on the watch's face and recorded a memo. "And what will you be doing?" he asked when he'd finished.

"Officially? I just got notified that one of the guys at my Cleveland bar is sick and I'm headed there to cover for him. If you need to get in touch with me, let any of the bartenders here know." Jake grinned. "How much you tip them tells them how urgent it is. I hope the agency gives you enough cash to handle contingencies."

"What will you really be doing?"

"Staying in the background so she'll never see me. If

you spot me—and you won't unless I want you to—get somewhere private and I'll come to you."

Houck reached into his pocket and flashed his badge. "You're testing my patience, Mr. Hennessey. I'm a trained professional and you're nothing but a small-town James Bond wanna-be. My job is on the line, and I won't let a barkeeper mess things up."

Jake clasped his hands under his chin and leaned on them, staring at Houck until the agent dropped his gaze. "I don't give a damn about your badge or your job. The only thing that's important is Harmony's safety. We don't have to like each other, but we are going to need to cooperate. Are you professional enough to handle it?"

Chapter 2

Jake sat in his beat-up beige sedan down the block from Harmony's house. He didn't like working without a plan and didn't have time to come up with one. He chewed over his options.

His normal contacts couldn't help—they were fine for quick and easy jobs, but nothing this complicated. Besides, he wouldn't involve them in anything that would put their lives at risk.

The small lights that highlighted the base of the front of the house provided a warm glow, but there were motion-activated security lights hidden among them. Another set of sensors nestled among the gingerbreading that decorated all three floors. Alarms protected the windows on the first and second floors.

There was one weak spot. Several years back, heavy rains had flooded the sensor on the basement door and put it out of commission. Eli had always planned on fixing it. He never did.

As a temporary measure, Jake had replaced it with a fake alarm. He switched out the batteries twice a year, so it still blinked a warning to intruders.

It was an easy fix. He'd call in a few favors and get the back of the house watched twenty-four hours a day. They wouldn't have to confront anyone, just text him if they spotted anything suspicious.

A white SUV cruised down the street and Jake craned his neck to see who was driving, but the closest streetlight was blown out. He added two items to his list: bribe his contact with city maintenance to come out and replace the light, and find out what kind of car Houck drove.

He didn't see any vehicle parked nearby that looked government-issued. Either Houck was very good, or he'd ignored Jake's advice about becoming Harmony's shadow. Jake was willing to wait before passing judgment.

A light rain spattered against the windshield, and Jake pulled a blanket from the back seat and covered himself. Even though there was no light inside the house, which meant Harmony was sleeping, he'd spend the night watching over her. It was the best he could do.

❄ ❄ ❄

The Oak Grove police station had never been a friendly place, and today was no exception. Jake studied the flow of people entering and leaving. Not the normal mix of citizens seeking to file a complaint and grim-faced cops, but somber people dressed in black, leaving flowers at an impromptu memorial on the sidewalk by the front door. They were there to honor the memory of the late police chief. The many-colored blossoms created an oddly cheerful contrast to the dingy gray building.

He stood propped against his car, arms crossed, waiting for the one cop who would listen to him: Harmony's old friend, Detective Fred Thomason. Jake had a well-deserved aversion to the cop shop and didn't want to go inside. If he stood there long enough, he'd make someone nervous, and they would come check him out. It wouldn't take long on a normal day. Today wasn't normal, and it would take every bit of patience he had.

Ten minutes in, an officer that often patrolled near the bar exited the station and acknowledged Jake with a chin jerk, which Jake returned. Twenty minutes in, another cop stood in the front door and studied Jake for a long moment. Five minutes later, the second one was back, and the frown on his face told Jake he was seriously annoyed.

The cop strode across the street, not even looking both ways, with his hand on his waist near his holster. He stopped a few feet away and pointed a finger, almost touching Jake's chest. "Do you have a problem?"

Jake spread his arms open. "No problem at all. I'm hoping to talk to Detective Thomason, but I don't want to interfere with the proceedings."

"I'll convey the message, but won't give you any guarantees."

"Fair enough. Tell him it has to do with Harmony Duprie."

There had been a time when every local cop knew Harmony. Hell, there had been a time when he knew most of them. Now, even with a smaller force, he might recognize the faces but not the names. From the way this one's eyebrows crunched together, he had no clue who Harmony was.

"He'll know," Jake said.

It only took three minutes before Thomason, a brown-haired man of average height, appeared in the doorway. Jake didn't bump into him often, but the only thing that ever changed about him was the thickness of his glasses. His and Jake's eyes met across the street. Then the detective was stopped by a trio of mourners. It took him five minutes to deal with them and get to Jake.

Thomason held out his hand. "Haven't seen you for awhile."

"I consider that a good thing." Jake grinned as they shook. "This is for Harmony, so I have to break the streak."

"I heard she came to town for Chief Sorenson's funeral."

In an unspoken but mutual agreement, they walked north, their footsteps in unconscious unison.

"She got in late yesterday." Jake bent to pick up a fast-food wrapper, then tossed it in a nearby trash can. "She brought a shadow with her."

Thomason stopped. "What kind of shadow?"

"He says he's with a small federal agency—FASS. I don't have a way to verify his credentials." Jake reached in his pocket and pulled out the agent's business card, handing it to Thomason. "He claims he's been in touch with local officials."

"No one mentioned it to me." The detective's eyes narrowed as he studied the card. "Either he's lying, or Chief Santos is holding out on me."

"Maybe the chief thinks you're too close to Angel to be analytical about the problem," Jake said as they resumed walking.

"Or he hasn't forgiven me for being the top candidate for the chief position when Sorenson retired five years ago. It amazed lots of people when I turned it down, Santos among them." Thomason grinned. "I think he's still afraid I'll change my mind and go gunning for the spot. And you never heard me say that."

Jake nodded. "Of course not. Where does that leave us?"

Thomason stopped again. "We'll have to keep it unofficial. There are enough of the retired guys in town who remember Harmony to give her coverage at the funeral itself. I might talk a few of them into patrolling near her house and keeping an eye on things. If their wives don't have other plans, that is."

"If you cover the front, I'm setting up some guys to hang out in the woods out back."

"And what about the Fed?"

"He's all yours." Jake flashed his brightest smile. "No offense, but you law-enforcement types make me nervous."

Thomason snorted. "Don't feed me that line. I'll deal with him. Who do I tell my contacts to watch for?"

Jake opened his arms and turned in a circle. "Everyone. Houck didn't share that information."

"Is he with Harmony now?"

"Houck? I didn't see him this morning and I'm not happy about it. Gloria, from the cleaning company, went over with the excuse of having work to finish. She served in the military and has skill in combat situations. How long Angel will play along is another question."

"What are you going to do?"

It wasn't the first time he'd done something like this, but never on this scale.

"Call in every favor anyone owes me. Search every corner of this city. Find a way to protect her, no matter what it takes."

❈ ❈ ❈

"You expect me to show up at Sorenson's funeral?" Tiny, the 320-pound owner of The Outlaw, Oak Grove's oldest biker bar, laughed. "Not likely."

"Like the authorities will let either of us anywhere near the service." Jake shook his head. "What I'm after is information. Who in town has a motive to hurt Harmony?"

"That's a big ask, considering I don't like you. And in less than twenty-four hours, it's about impossible."

Jake let the ghost of a smile cross his lips. "You don't have to pussyfoot around. I know you think I stole The Purple Onion from you. I hope you'll put your feelings for me aside and do this for Harmony. You were in the same class in high school, right?"

Tiny's eyes widened. "You've done your homework. Hell, we even went on a date. She was too much of a straight-arrow for me."

"So, you'll do what you can?"
"For her? Count me in."

By noon, Jake had visited four more bars and gotten promises of help from all of them. An hour later, he'd made a trip to a shopping mall north of Pittsburgh to pick up supplies. Two hours after that, he'd rented an old car, dyed his hair, changed into a new wardrobe—faded, torn jeans and an oversized Steelers T-shirt—and topped it off with a pair of thick, fake glasses. The one thing he didn't do was pick up a burner phone. He wanted his army of volunteers to be able to reach him.

And reports had been coming in. Janine and Sarah, two of Harmony's old friends, had visited. The mail service delivered a package, after clearing it with the retired cop out front. The flowers Jake sent anonymously had shown up. She hadn't left the house, which made Jake happy.

Houck hadn't made an appearance either. Jake wondered again if the agent was very good or that bad.

By four in the afternoon, Jake was back in The Outlaw, having a beer and listening to gossip. Although he earned his share of glances, no one bothered him. Even Tiny didn't recognize him.

That was his only success. There was lots of talk about the funeral, but no gossip about any threat to Harmony.

He moved on to Mama D's for supper, even though Mama D had retired and lived in Florida now. Her distant cousin Vinnie had taken over, and the quality of the food had gone downhill, but it was still a good place to catch up on the rumor mill. Years ago, it had been one of Harmony's favorite places. A part of him hoped she'd show up.

He was done with his supper and hadn't picked up any useful information. Was the threat nothing more than Houck's imagination? There was one other theory to consider; this was a trap, and he was the target.

Chapter 3

Jake had lived with a bulls-eye on his back ever since the time he got caught shoplifting a pair of expensive jeans as a twelve-year-old. Because he never made it out of the store, and it was a first offense, he had gotten off with a warning, but he had also made it onto the blacklist with the local cops. He learned a lot from that experience—about how to not get caught.

The first rule was never steal from a store where he'd need to shop later. As an adult, he'd extended that rule to include the city where he lived. Which meant Oak Grove was off limits, and local officials had no interest in his activities.

Once in a blue moon, a newly hatched FBI agent stumbled across old files and got the notion Jake was the path to establishing their reputation. None of them were more than an inconvenience until their superior called off the hunt. And Harmony had never been dragged into their wild goose chases before.

After paying his bill, Jake stood in the doorway of Mama D's while he pulled on his jacket and studied the minimal traffic. The light rain glittered in the streetlights and danced on the pavement. His phone dinged with an incoming message, and he rushed to the shelter of the rental car before retrieving it.

"*Supper delivered*," it read. "*She has company. The real estate lady. The librarian. Thomason.*"

That was the best Jake could have hoped for. Thomason and Sarah, the real estate friend, were married. They were built in security without it being obvious.

That gave Jake a two or three-hour window for a nap. Or at least an hour and a half, and time to cruise through Angel's neighborhood a few times. It bothered him that no one had heard from or spotted Houck.

The curtains in her house were closed, although light leaked through the cracks. A police cruiser sat in the driveway, confirmation of Thomason's presence. The cops drove official vehicles in town, even when on personal business, to make it appear their numbers were larger than the payroll showed. Jake assumed the additional car he didn't recognize belonged to Janine, Oak Grove's head librarian.

He pulled onto the side street and studied the various cars parked nearby. None of them were the standard black, government-issued sedan.

There were other ways to identify cars with occupants. He scanned the vehicles for one with fogged-up windows and came up empty. No cigarette ember trails anywhere, either.

He caught a spark of light in the third-story window of the house across the street from Harmony's. The empty house. The one Jake was waiting to come on the market to buy and remodel. It had only been a flash, but he'd seen it.

There were two possibilities: Houck or the unknown threat.

Jake didn't have a key to the old house. He didn't need one, but getting past the squeaky floorboards and to the attic unnoticed would be a challenge for his rusty skills.

He turned off the car's overhead light so it wouldn't turn on as he eased out the passenger door, where he was less likely to be noticed. Then he dashed to the sparse cover provided by a nearby azalea. From there, Jake worked his way down the alley, counting the houses so he didn't break into the wrong one.

The black sedan parked in the yard was the first sign he was at the right place. The government plates were the dead giveaway and all he needed for confirmation.

The thrill of the chase surged through his blood. In a crouch, he eased his way past an abandoned bicycle and to the back door. Jake hoped it was locked. It would be fun to pick it using only items he found nearby.

A trial twist of the doorknob dashed his hopes. It turned easily, and the door opened with the smallest push and the slightest of creaks. Jake peeked through the crack and saw nothing more than a kitchen littered with trash, the remains of not cleaning after the owner moved out. He should have stopped there.

He didn't.

Two steps in, he stood and waited for his eyes to adjust. Then he inched through the kitchen, avoiding dinged-up pots and cracked plastic containers.

He paused at the base of the stairs. A car's tires squealed as it made the turn too fast on the wet pavement, but the house was silent. No clock ticked. No faucet dripped. The old wooden steps presented a risk—one creak at the wrong moment and the game would be over.

His back to the wall and his feet pressed against the baseboard, Jake took one cautious step at a time up the stairs. The fourth one groaned as he shifted his full weight onto it. He stopped, listening for any sounds from overhead, but there was no response. He waited for his breath to return to a slow, steady pace and continued upward.

There was no staircase to the attic. Instead, a wooden ladder had been lowered from the ceiling. Not what he wanted, but he was too close to give up. He leaned on the ladder to judge its trustworthiness and was surprised at its sturdiness.

This was the most dangerous part. If Houck came down as Jake was going up, there'd be no escape. He planted his foot on the bottom rung and started the climb.

With his head still below the floor of the third story, he reached into his pocket and pulled out his phone. He was slipping—he should have turned off the flash for the camera earlier. With the phone's screen shaded by his jacket, he changed the setting, so he was free to snap as many photos as he wanted.

Then, as he raised his arm to take a picture while remaining unseen, he figured out the flaw in his plan. If he caught Houck in the shot, all he'd get was the back of the agent's head. Assuming, of course, that Houck was staring out the window, keeping an eye on Harmony's house. Or did an array of instruments maintain surveillance while Houck snuck in a nap?

This wasn't going to be a precision operation. Jake raised his arm and used the burst feature to take a series of pictures. With luck, he'd get at least one useful photo.

He traced his steps back to the first floor and took a moment to review the pictures. A snap of the side of the man's face identified him as Houck. Another shot revealed how outdated his equipment was. Not that Jake was an expert, but he monitored the black market and had been offered a few of the newer instruments.

The setup was adequate for surveillance, but no good for protecting Harmony. If someone mounted a sudden attack, Houck wouldn't make it to the first floor before the damage was done.

Not that Jake could do any better. He didn't carry a gun.

Jake needed to update Thomason, but he couldn't walk in the front door and announce himself. He and Sarah had worked on real estate deals in the past, and he had her number in his contacts. He sent her a text. *"Don't let Harmony know. Ask your husband to meet me in the backyard in five."*

The response came back sooner than he expected. "*He's on his way.*"

Jake closed the kitchen door behind himself. He scurried through the alley until he reached the street, then casually strolled down the sidewalk, just a man out for a walk. The trunk of an old oak provided cover to hop the back fence without being spotted. A series of mountain laurels gave him the cover he needed to get closer to the house.

Fifteen feet lay between the last bush and the back door, and ten feet to the edge of the range for the security lights. With perfect timing, he'd gotten as close as possible as Thomason came out of the back door with a bag of garbage. The interior lights framed him, making him an easy target, but Jake didn't want to shoot him.

"Hey, Thomason," he called quietly.

The detective automatically reached for his gun, then let his hand drop. "Hennessey."

Jake rose from behind the bush. "Here."

"Holy . . . that's impressive." Thomason strode to Jake's hiding spot. "We'll discuss the change in your appearance later. What's going on?"

"Any official word on Houck?"

"Only that there are several Feds in town. No details. They've frozen me out."

"I can help. He's maintaining surveillance from the attic of the vacant house across the street." Jake flipped through the photo gallery to the right picture, then handed his phone to the cop. "It's not a great picture, but it's the best I could do."

Thomason studied the photo. "How did you get this?"

"He left the back door unlocked." Jake raised his right hand. "Swear to God."

"Do you mind if I send this to myself?"

It was Jake's business cell phone, and the number appeared in various city and state records. "Go for it. Will you get in trouble for going around Santos' back?"

One side of Thomason's mouth rose. "Probably. I'll do it for the same reason as you're skirting the edge of legality—Harmony."

"She has that effect on people." Jake rubbed his neck. "How is she doing? I mean, really doing?"

"I'm a cop. A good one. I'm trained to see when people are lying. And every time she opens her mouth, she's lying." Thomason handed the phone back to Jake and stuck his hands in his pockets.

"She's saying all the right words," he continued. "But hesitates before answering questions, as if she needs to figure out what people want to hear. She glances away even when she answers a question as simple as 'How are you?' When she thinks no one is watching, she slumps, as if it's too much effort to stand up straight. I'm not a psychiatrist, and I don't know how to help her or if she'll admit she needs help."

Thomason shook his head. "The tough part is, we can't allow any of this to distract us until we know she is safe."

Jake knew a lot about lying, including how to cover it up so no one could tell. He stared Thomason straight in the eyes, willing the detective to believe him. "She's an old friend, nothing more. I just want her to be safe."

❄ ❄ ❄

That's why he half -lay across the front seat of the rental car, leaning against the passenger-side window, wrapped in a blanket, and fighting back sleep. The librarian had left a couple of hours ago, and Thomason and Sarah weren't far behind, although the cop hung around the porch as long as possible. Longer than polite. Sarah had eventually forced him to the car, and they had left after circling the block. Twice.

Jake regretted he couldn't monitor both Harmony's house and Houck's hiding spot from the same vantage point. He would have liked to know if Houck got any visitors, and who they were.

At a quarter after two, his cell phone vibrated. It was Danny, checking in with the night's report from the bar.

Jake answered with no greeting. "How'd things go?"

"Slow night. I talked with friends at a couple of other bars, and they said the same thing. The city brought in help from the sheriff's department and nearby towns in case anyone wanted to interfere with the funeral. So, almost everyone went home early. They didn't want to risk getting stopped. Hell, the only thing anyone drank after midnight was coffee. You're going to have to increase your coffee order if this keeps up."

Jake's policy decreed coffee was always free after midnight. He'd probably lost money. "I hope they tipped, at least."

Danny chuckled. "Wilson came in, hoping for the latest gossip. He made sure everyone expressed their appreciation. I could have handled the night by myself, but I let Rene stay until close."

Rene was one of the part-time bartenders. "That's

fine," Jake said. "I prefer having two staff in the building."

"Right. How are things going on your end?"

"Dead. Which, in this case, is good. This looks like an exercise in futility, made up to justify somebody's job." Jake paused. "But this is Harmony we're talking about. She's always had the uncanny ability to attract trouble."

Danny yawned. "Right. So, let me get the place closed and I'll plan on opening in the morning. Call me if you need me."

"I will. Thanks." Jake hung up, laid the phone down, and blinked to allow his eyes to adjust to the darkness. A police car cruised by, and he was tempted to go home and get some sleep. It didn't look like anything would happen.

He felt indirectly responsible for the current state of events. Maybe if he hadn't intruded in Harmony's life in the first place, those twenty-five plus years ago, none of this would be happening now. He pulled the blanket up to his shoulders and settled in for a long night.

Chapter 4

The remembrance ceremony for Chief Sorenson was scheduled for eleven a.m. at the high school gymnasium. It would be the biggest event in Oak Grove since the annual spring Bird Watching Festival. None of the churches in town were large enough to hold the expected crowd. Jake would have liked to pay his respects to Sorenson, who'd been a good cop, and understood life wasn't always black or white.

Jake's focus needed to remain on Harmony. Sarah had shown up at the Victorian house at ten a.m. to take her to the service. The four retired cops stayed out of sight until Harmony was outside and it was too late for her to back out. From his position down the street, Jake hadn't been able to see Harmony's face, only that she was dressed in black. All he'd had to gauge her reaction was a stiffening of her spine, the lifting of her head. Had she even known she was being guarded?

They hustled her into the second of three cars, like they would a celebrity. The small motorcade drove away from the neighborhood. Still, Jake couldn't relax.

A shortcut of side streets and alleys got him across town to his apartment in record time. After a fast shower and changing into a suit, Jake walked towards the high school, planning to keep an eye on the proceedings by mingling with the crowd outside. He had to trust the official law enforcement presence to protect Harmony. Not that they'd been any good at it two years ago.

"Look at you, all dressed up," said a woman's voice from behind him.

He stopped to allow Eddie to catch up. "I didn't think anyone would recognize me."

"I've admired that view from the back more than once." A broad smile lit her face. "The giveaway is that little limp. How'd'ya get it?"

In a nearly failed heist and a too-close encounter with a determined cop. Not that he'd ever tell anyone. "A keg fell on my foot years ago. Didn't bother me then, but as I got older, the damage showed. It gets worse as the weather turns colder."

Eddie nodded and rubbed her right elbow. "Yeah, I call this my weathervane. Starts hurting before big storms. Anyway, I'm glad I ran into you. Got some news. I was gonna pass the word to Danny, but now I can tell you."

"You won the lottery?"

"I wish. Naw, I picked up some extra hours this morning. Different batch of customers than I usually deal with. Not a problem, but two of them gave me the creeps. They acted like they'd never been in a convenience store before, picking up weird things, laughing about them, and putting them back."

Vague enough to set off alarms while being almost useless. "What did they look like?"

"Taller than me, shorter than you." Eddie frowned as she thought. "Brown hair, short but not a crew cut. They were wearing jeans, but new ones. Stiff. Not even washed yet. That's what bothered me. They were trying to look casual, and it wasn't working. I was too busy ringing up sales to get a picture of them."

They didn't fit the standard profile of customers of a convenience store on the wrong side of the tracks in Oak Grove. Jake took a folded-up bill from his wallet and handed it to Eddie. "You did good. Got any clue what country they might have come from?"

She shook her head. "I know just enough Spanish to know that's not what they were speaking. Anything else would be guessing."

"I appreciate your help." Jake slipped his arm around her waist and kissed her on the cheek. "Now, do me a favor. Head home and stay out of trouble until the funeral is over, okay?"

"And don't ask too many questions. Got it. Stay safe, Hennessey."

It wasn't enough information to pass on to Thomason or Houck. Jake scanned the small gathering of people outside the school, anyway. He recognized most of the faces, and no one fit the description from Eddie. Most of the spectators wore their Sunday-go-to-meeting clothes as a sign of respect.

The school had canceled classes for the day, so numerous teenagers hung around, waiting for the spectacle. Krunk was there. He studied Jake's face and nodded, then turned away. If Jake needed him, he'd be close by. Several of the bar regulars had shown up, but they were busy chatting with each other and didn't pay any attention to him. Which was what he wanted.

Sirens heralded the arrival of a procession of cop cars and motorcycles, some from as far away as West Virginia and Chicago. A chain of black limos followed them. The hearse entered last and pulled up to the main entrance of the gymnasium. In an orderly parade, the pall bearers escorted Chief Sorenson's coffin inside, leading the way for everyone else to follow.

Jake didn't spot Harmony among the arrivals, but it seemed they'd only included the big shots in the procession. Dread rose in his chest. He casually asked the man nearest to him, "Where are all the locals that were invited? I didn't see my neighbor. I hope nothing went wrong."

"The news report I saw last night said they were supposed to park on the other side of the school and use the back door. Something about avoiding a traffic jam." The middle-aged man frowned and jerked his chin towards the road where several news trucks recorded the proceedings. "I heard a rumor that a celebrity showed up and they wanted to hide him from the reporters. That can't be right, because what big name would show their face in Oak Grove?"

Harmony wasn't a celebrity, but there were several reasons she wouldn't want her face to show up on camera. Even if the traffic flow story was a cover, it made sense. Jake wished he'd known ahead of time. He'd been hoping to catch a glimpse of her and check that the plan for her security was working.

Now that he considered it, there were probably many ways to gain entrance to the school and the gym. Jake swore under his breath. He was slipping—he'd allowed his personal feelings to get in the way of treating this like a job.

He pulled his attention away from the last of the mourners entering the school and assessed the situation. The four men standing in a huddle near the gate were too obvious. All Feds, and Houck was one of them. So, Houck had wrangled up some reinforcements. Jake weighed his options—wait for them to spread out and then approach Houck or throw himself into the pit of lions. The third option, to ignore them, gained him nothing.

With slow, deliberate steps, he walked toward them, giving them time to adjust to his presence. Houck's eyes narrowed, then widened. Jake stopped fifteen feet away and waited for Houck to close the gap.

"Where have you been?" Houck snapped.

"Good morning to you, too, Special Agent." Jake casually tugged the cuffs of his shirt to straighten them. "I told you I would find you if I had information to share. Which, unfortunately, I don't."

"You should have let me know about the people you hired to guard Mrs. Hennessey."

"Mrs. Duprie-Hennessey," Jake corrected. "It is important to her to keep her family name. And I didn't hire anyone. They are volunteers. She holds a special place in this town's heart."

"Or her money does," Houck muttered.

Whatever minimal respect Jake might have given Houck fled. He carefully schooled his face to be expressionless. "You got backup. Does that mean you received additional intelligence?"

"Ther're not for her. Are you familiar with Senator Hawkins? She caught wind of the funeral and dropped in to pay her respects. They," Houck jerked his chin towards the three other agents, "are part of her Secret Service contingent. A totally last-minute arrangement. They received an hour's notice before the flight into Pittsburgh."

Which explained why Jake hadn't caught wind of it. "She's running on a law-and-order platform, right? Maybe their presence scared off the group targeting Harmony."

Houck nodded. "Or in a worse-case scenario, delayed their attack. And I don't know how long we'll have a budget to continue protection."

Leaving her defenseless. "What can you do to make Harmony a priority?"

Houck shrugged. "I need more than vague rumors. I need solid intelligence. And it's just not there."

Waiting outside for the service to end and the procession to head to the cemetery, like a groupie waiting for a rock star, didn't appeal to Jake. With Houck and the other agents on duty, he wasn't needed. So he started the walk back to his apartment. The stroll would give him time to clear his mind and formulate a long-term plan.

The route he chose reminded him of the town's

downfall. Houses in need of paint and repairs, rusted cars on blocks in the driveways, empty plastic bags and other litter blowing around. He grabbed one bag, intending to fill it with garbage and find a place to dispose of it. Harmony had shamed him into starting the practice once upon a time.

The back streets of Oak Grove were always quiet, but on this day there were fewer cars than normal. Still, Jake kept an eye on the traffic. An old habit, born of watching for the police. The cops were busy in other parts of town.

When the same car passed him twice, it caught his attention. It didn't come back for a third look, and he rationalized the driver was probably lost and looking for an address. It snapped him out of the sense of security the walk had lulled him into. That's why he noticed an annoying buzzing growing louder. One of those electric motorcycles, he guessed. There were lots around town. He missed the rumble of the old-fashioned bikes.

He turned at the moment the bike gunned its way onto the sidewalk. Jake didn't have time to get out of the way.

Chapter 5

Everything hurt.

That was despite the pain meds Trina, the nurse—a heavy-set, black-haired lady—had given Jake. Even a shot of whiskey wouldn't help at this point. She was out in the hallway having a loud discussion with two men. Actually, she was yelling at them, but Jake couldn't hear their side of the disagreement. Something about needing a place to stay and Pittsburgh. Maybe his mind was still muddled from the accident. He just wanted to go home.

The door opened, and he forced open his eyes, expecting to see Trina.

"Got yourself in a world of hurt, didn't you?" Detective Thomason asked.

Jake pulled the thin blanket over his chest. "Scrapes, bruises, and apparently a broken arm. Still waiting for confirmation from Doc Gabe."

"Do you mind if I ask you a few questions while you wait?"

"Fire away." Jake winced. "Do me a favor and stand

where I can see you. They have my neck immobilized as a precaution."

Thomason moved to the end of the bed. "We got the basic details from an old lady who was in her yard raking leaves, so we just need things from your point of view."

"It was the weirdest thing. All I was doing was walking down the sidewalk, headed home. I'd talked to a couple of people at the high school, including Special Agent Houck, and that was it. There's no doubt in my mind it was deliberate."

"What did the bike rider look like?" the detective asked.

"Black jeans, black jacket, a black helmet with a mirrored visor. All I saw when I turned around was my face reflecting back at me."

"You make any new enemies recently?"

Jake blinked several times. "Not that I'm aware of. I haven't changed suppliers, haven't made any new business deals. My attention has been focused on Harmony."

Thomason grimaced. "I'm speculating that the attack on you is tied to her. We've been unable to find any trace of the rider or the motorcycle, but it would be easy enough for someone to slip out of town by mixing in with people leaving the memorial service."

"Is Houck keeping an eye on her?"

"Yes, and he's using the attack as justification for added support." One side of Thomason's mouth rose. "He's also made an official request that I be assigned as his liaison. Santos isn't happy, but he's given in to the pressure."

"Any luck with security cameras in the area?"

Thomason chuckled. "You're thinking like a cop, Hennessey."

No, Jake was thinking like a robber who had to stay one step ahead of the cops. "Is that supposed to be a compliment?"

He shifted, trying to find a comfortable position on the hard hospital-type bed. With his left arm restrained, waiting for a potential cast, it was impossible.

"We've got Jenkins going door to door," Thomason continued, ignoring the question. "But they don't trust the police. There's a rash of out-of-order home cameras. Even when she mentions your name, no one wants to talk."

"They go to the same church, home-school their kids, and aren't my customers. They don't know who I am."

"That's all I know about them, too. From what I've been told, they're almost a cult with ties to a little country overseas. I forget the name."

"Shit!" Jake struggled to sit up.

Thomason gently pushed Jake's chest until he was flat on his back again. "I'll handle the investigation. Trina?" he called.

The nurse sauntered into the room and surveyed the situation. "Mr. Hennessey giving you a hard time, Detective?"

"No, but I'm going to step outside to make a call. I wanted to make sure someone was keeping an eye on him."

"No worries. We received the okay to treat his arm with a splint for now. We'll keep him busy. Go make your call."

"No cast?" Jake asked hopefully, as Trina fussed with the wraps on his arm.

"I didn't say that. The doc is going to splint and bandage your arm and check it tomorrow to see how the swelling is doing. He won't put a cast on for a day or two."

"I guess I won't be moving kegs around for a few weeks." Or carrying off any heists. Good thing he didn't have one planned.

❉ ❉ ❉

I can call Danny to give me a lift if the bar isn't busy, Jake thought, as he waited for the final set of X-rays to be read. *Rene can handle things by himself for a few minutes.*

The doc had done a fine job of securing his arm. The pain medicine had finally kicked in and left him feeling all right. It was better than a shot of aged whiskey. He hadn't seen Thomason since he left to make his phone call, and Jake wished he'd gotten an update. Of course, Jake had been a bit preoccupied.

Trina stuck her head into the treatment room. "You doing okay in here?"

He successfully raised himself on his right elbow. "Ready to go home. Where did my clothes get to?"

"You don't remember, do you?" She grabbed a bag from a table. "The accident destroyed them. Your cell phone survived, but we turned it off so it wouldn't disturb us."

"May I have it? I need to call a friend and see if they can pick me up."

"Can you stay with your friend? The doc doesn't want you to be by yourself tonight. You know the clinic doesn't stay open at night anymore. He was talking about seeing if the nursing home in town would put you up for a night or two, as a precaution."

That sounded like Jake's definition of hell. Stuck in a smelly little room without his own clothes, terrible food, no booze, and a bunch of old people vying for his attention. "Is that really necessary?"

She didn't get a chance to answer because there was a light rap on the door and Thomason strode in.

"Sorry to interrupt, Trina, but do you mind if I have a word with Hennessey in private? Official police business."

Jake's heart rate shot up. He'd done nothing wrong, but it was an automatic reflex. He'd had too many close calls with cops in his alternative life. "What's up, Detective?" he asked, trying to sound casual.

Thomason pulled a chair up to the bed, sitting in it backwards and resting his forearms on the back, as he waited for Trina to leave the room, shutting the door on her way out. "Have you seen yourself in a mirror yet?"

"I've had other things to worry about." The question had Jake wondering. *How bad is it?*

"Houck wants to put you in a safe house. I told him you wouldn't agree."

Jake nodded. "I have businesses to run."

"It might be a good idea for you to go stay in Cleveland. Do you have anyone there you trust?"

"They wouldn't be working for me if I didn't trust them. But I can't leave Oak Grove while Harmony is in danger."

The detective rested his chin on his arms. "I figured that would be your reaction. I considered offering to have you stay with me, but I won't let Sarah be part of this."

"What do you think 'this' is?"

"It would be easy to blame everything on the group on Birch Street. My cop sense says no. They've lived here for ten years, and have never been a problem. Sure, the women wear old-fashioned clothes and they keep to themselves, but there's nothing wrong with that."

"I can't believe a group would move here just to set up a scenario where Harmony might show up and they'd get a chance to attack her." Jake shifted on the bed, tired of lying there.

Thomason nodded. "It seems farfetched. Houck claims there have been instances of twenty years of infiltration before carrying out an operation. He couldn't cite any because of security, but I feel like it's a myth passed on in their training. We have to consider the possibility the attack has nothing to do with Harmony. The timing was a coincidence."

Jake's eyebrows lifted. "You know what she would say about that."

"You mean that there's no such thing as coincidence?" Thomason shook his head. "It would be easier if we got Harmony involved. Let her do her magic of analyzing the data. Figure out what she can see that other people are missing. But Houck doesn't want to alarm her."

The Towers—once the best hotel in Oak Grove—was

now, like the city, a shadow of its old self. The carpets were worn but clean; the walls dinged by the passing of countless luggage carts, and the bathroom fixtures were out of date. The view from the top floor still held a touch of magic. In his darkened room, Jake stared at the streetlights and wondered what he'd missed.

He'd made the arrangement as a compromise with Thomason and Houck. He'd stay at the hotel for two nights or more, depending on how his follow-up appointments with the doctor went. That would give the authorities time to find his attacker.

Jake had no intention of sticking to the agreement. He'd memorized the location of every exterior door and how to get to them without triggering an alarm. Webb, at the front desk was Danny's nephew, and had figured out how to make the security system blip on command.

Tonight, Jake wasn't going anywhere. He needed to soak in the tub with the water as hot as he could stand it while resting his arm on the edge. It wouldn't improve his looks, but might ease the pain from the bruises that covered him from head to foot.

That would happen after Webb brought him the food Jake had ordered from the diner down the street. Mary, who took the order, had been known to drop by The Purple Onion on her nights off. Neither of them would reveal where he was.

Jake turned on the TV and sat on the end of the bed while he waited. In the semi-darkness, he dug a burner cell phone out of the duffel bag Danny had brought his clothes in, the one he kept in the office as a 'go' bag. The battery and SIM card were in two different pockets.

He wouldn't turn it on yet. His business cell phone had survived the attack, but Jake had switched the ringer to silent. He wasn't hiding from law enforcement. They knew his location.

Someone knocked on the door. Three raps, a pause, and another knock—it must be Webb with the food. The timing was perfect, because his stomach rumbled. Jake looked out the peephole, anyway. Yep, Webb.

He turned on the lights, opened the door, and stepped away, making room for Webb to carry in the food. Under other circumstances, he would have paid more attention to the frown on the lanky young man's face. But Jake was tired, hungry and hurting again. It was easy to make a mistake.

"I'm sorry," Webb said.

"For what?" Jake asked as he dug into his wallet for cash for a tip. It was hard to do with only one hand.

"I couldn't stop her."

Jake glanced up. "Stop who?"

"I should kill you, Jake Hennessey," a woman said. "But it looks like someone already tried."

Chapter 6

It was the moment that Jake had dreaded and longed for, but he wasn't ready for it. He avoided acknowledging Harmony and took the time to hand Webb a tip. Webb didn't wait for the fireworks and closed the door of the hotel room on his way out, leaving Jake trapped.

She's not the enemy, he reminded himself. "Hello, Angel."

"Hello, Angel," she mimicked him. "Twenty-some years and that's all you have to say?"

"Have a seat." He pulled out the only chair in the room. "Or take the bed. Your pick. I need to sit."

She eyed him and the bed, then limped to the chair. The hem of her black, wide-legged pants grazed across the carpet. "Sit before you fall. You look terrible, by the way, despite the disguise. That doesn't mean I'm going to take pity on you."

"Not even a little?" He tried to smile as he collapsed onto the sagging mattress.

"When you disappeared and left me wondering if you'd fled the country or were dead?" She banged her cane against the end of the bed.

Jake wasn't sure he could have this conversation without the aid of a liberal amount of alcohol. which he'd neglected to procure while gathering his supplies. "Twenty-two."

"Twenty-two what?"

"Twenty-two years since the last time we talked. At your and Eli's wedding. When the representatives of four different government agencies informed me in no uncertain terms that they would make my life miserable if I didn't end any form of contact with you and Eli."

Her jaw dropped. "What?"

"I let Eli know, of course, and we found ways to stay in touch that they couldn't track. It was his decision not to tell you."

"He never said anything." She stood and limped over to the window.

Jake got up and turned off the lights, so she wouldn't be visible from outside. "Security," he said. But he had heard sniffles and wanted to give her a resemblance of privacy.

"Who's after you, Jake?" she asked after a long moment.

"How did you find out about the attack, Angel?"

She didn't turn to face him. "Those retired cops who were my honor guard? They were listening to the police band on their phones. It was quite the shock when I figured out the chatter was about you. I pretended not to listen."

"I'm sorry." For many things. His words covered a lot of ground.

"I had to come and see you with my own eyes." She

turned around to face him. "What's going on, Jake?"

"I'm not the right person for you to discuss this with."

"Who is?"

It was his turn to gaze out the window. Where was Houck? How had Harmony gotten to the hotel without the agent following her?

"Jake?" she prompted.

"Are you hungry, Angel? I won't be able to eat everything." He closed the curtains before turning the light back on.

"Avoiding the question?"

"Yes. I'm not sure how much I'm allowed to say." Using his good hand, Jake pulled the food containers from the bag, and arranged them on the dresser. "You've dealt with these security types for years, you understand."

"I haven't done a job for the government since… my security clearance is probably inactive. Not that it matters. I won't be working for any of the agencies again. My plans are to find a little house in Oak Grove and settle into my position as a research librarian until I retire." She leaned heavily on the cane and hobbled back to the chair.

Something about the cane looked weird, like it wasn't put together right. He'd have to see if he could fix it. "I heard you were moving back. That's one thing that hasn't changed—the Oak Grove rumor mill."

He placed a container of soup with the other dishes. The lid was on tight, and he struggled to open it one-handed.

"Let me help." Harmony easily opened the lid and took a deep sniff. "Is this the Dairy Barn's homemade chicken noodle? Do you know how long it's been? Can I have some?"

He hadn't guessed food would distract her. "Help yourself. I've got my heart set on that burger."

It had been too long since he'd shared a meal with Harmony. This wasn't like old times with easy conversation, but it eased the tension between the two of them. Jake suspected it wouldn't last. There were too many secrets.

His phone buzzed. He didn't feel like standing and walking the few steps to retrieve it. "Will you toss that to me?"

As she picked it up, she glanced at the screen. "Freddie? Why is he calling you?"

"Detective Thomason is likely hoping I know where you are. What do you want me to tell him?"

She handed him the phone and rubbed her forehead. "Can you get me out of here without anyone knowing I was here?"

He answered the call. "Hold on, Thomason." Then he put it on mute. "Another time, Angel, it would be fun. Tonight, I'm not sneaking anywhere."

Jake took the phone off mute. "Sorry, I wanted to turn off the TV. What's up?. . . I ate. Now I'm going to take a hot bath. Any update on who attacked me? . . . Nothing, eh? No surprise. It would have been a miracle if you caught the guy this soon."

He listened intently, then nodded to Harmony and pushed the button to put the phone on speaker. "How did you let her get away?"

"What we didn't plan for," Thomason said, "is her

car can be remotely controlled. She sent it off to the convenience store a few blocks away and Brady, naturally, followed it. Then she called a ride share or something and took off while no one was watching. We're waiting for Houck to pull his tapes."

"Houck?" Harmony mouthed.

Jake nodded. "How can I help, Thomason? It's not like I can drive around town and look for her. Where would she go? Have you tried to call her?"

"She turned off her phone. We're triangulating against her last known signal. We'll track her down," Thomason promised.

"Keep me updated," Jake said. "I'll be here."

"How soon before Freddie shows up?" Harmony asked once the call was disconnected.

"Did you remember to take your SIM card out when you turned off your phone?"

Her eyes narrowed. "No, did I need to?"

"As long as your battery still holds a charge, it'll keep pinging the towers. My guess is that we have an hour or two before they find you. I can get Danny to come pick you up and take you somewhere, but we'll only be delaying the inevitable."

"Danny?" She tilted her head.

"My head bartender. Do you remember the bar, The Purple Onion? I own it now."

"You own a bar? Good for you. So, that's what you're doing in Oak Grove."

Jake nodded. "I also own a bar in Cleveland and split my time between them. They keep me busy and out of trouble." *At least as far as the authorities know.*

"It doesn't look like it to me." A smile lit her face for the first time since she'd walked in the door.

"Hey! Even I don't stand a chance against a motorcycle aimed straight at me."

Her smile disappeared. "How can I help, Jake? I still have a few contacts in law enforcement. I'll be glad to call them and see what they can do."

"Let Thomason handle it. If he needs help, he'll ask."

A loud knock on the door made both of them jump.

"That was faster than I expected. The police department must have got their hands on some new technology." Jake groaned as he stood. He'd stiffened up while eating. Out of habit, he peered out the peephole.

"Shit, that's not Thomason. Angel, are you aware of a government agency with the initials FASS?"

"I'm familiar with them. Why?"

"You're about to meet one of them. Special Agent Doan Houck, to be exact." Jake pulled open the door just as Houck raised his hand to knock again. "Guess who showed up," Jake said.

"Doan?" Harmony asked.

"Hello, Mrs. Duprie-Hennessey," Houck stepped into Jake's hotel room.

This wasn't what Jake had expected. He wasn't the only one keeping secrets. "You two know each other?"

"Doan works on the help desk. Or he did." She faced Houck. "What are you doing here? And what's this about being a special agent?" Harmony slowly stood, leaning on her cane.

"Is there somewhere we can talk in private?" Houck pushed the door closed halfway.

Jake returned to his spot on the bed. "If I'd known I was going to have company, I would have rented a suite. But what you see is what you get."

"And I won't ask Jake to leave his room." Harmony tipped her head towards Jake. "Besides, I'd like for him to hear what you say. Especially if it has anything to do with today's attack."

Houck scowled. "He's a security risk."

"I'm aware. Since I will never do another job for the U.S. government, I'm not worried about my clearance. He's also an old friend. I need his support." She poked Houck with her cane. "You can either grab a chair from the hall or stand. Your choice."

Jake expected the agent to argue, but Houck walked out of the room. "How long has Houck worked for the company?" Jake asked.

"Six months. He was incompetent at the job, but now I understand why he wasn't let go before his probation was over." Her lips formed a tight line. "Lando and Scotty are going to hear about this, going behind my back."

Jake had met the two men years ago when they'd come to Oak Grove to help Eli with a project. "I'm sure they had your best interests in mind. Let Houck explain his side of the story before you get too worked up."

"Nobody asks me what I think anymore," she grumbled.

Jake decided he needed to reveal his part of the setup before Houck did. "Angel," he started.

The door was shoved open, and Houck carried in a padded wooden chair. "This place has seen better days.

This is the first one I found that wasn't broken."

"The whole town has seen better times," Jake agreed. "At least the bar is hanging in there."

Houck put the chair down facing Harmony, then locked the door. "You couldn't convince me of that unless you showed me the books."

"Doan, sit. We're not here to talk about Jake's bar," Harmony interrupted. "Tell me what's going on."

"I was assigned to the case nine months ago." He perched on the edge of the chair. "The agency has been loosely keeping an eye on you, but didn't consider your case active. When one of our sister agencies stumbled across new information and shared it, they decided to reactivate your protection."

"From what, Doan?"

Houck stared at the floor. "The report is minimal, so we're treating it as a worst-case scenario."

"Meaning you assumed there's a threat to my life," Harmony said.

She sounded calm and in-charge, but she'd lost what little color was in her cheeks.

"We presumed something might happen at the funeral when you were alone and vulnerable. Between Hennessey, Thomason, and myself, you were well covered."

"So, the attack on Jake was revenge for not being able to get to me." Harmony glanced at Jake. "I'm sorry."

"I wouldn't jump to that conclusion so fast, Angel. Until we learn more about the people threatening you and who attacked me, we need to keep open minds."

She nodded but said nothing.

"What I'd like to do is to move into your house," Houck proposed. "It'll give me a better opportunity to deal with any lapse in security."

Jake stifled a smile and waited for the fireworks. Harmony didn't do bodyguards.

Chapter 7

Many years ago, Jake had insisted upon acting as a bodyguard for Harmony, even offering to spend the night on her landlords' closed-in porch, so he could make sure no one crept up the outside stairs to her apartment. She'd relented, and let him throw his sleeping bag on the floor of her front room. He'd hoped it was the first step to finding his way back into her bed, but that had never happened.

There'd been many times when he'd spent sleepless nights watching over her from a distance, times that she never knew about. Houck didn't stand a chance at getting her to let him move in with her.

When she didn't answer Houck's question immediately, Jake wondered if she'd lost her will to fight. He fluffed a pillow from the hotel room's bed and stuck it between his lap and his sling to give his injured arm extra support.

"I'll put my equipment and a cot in the den," Houck continued, not waiting for Harmony's acquiescence.

From the pattern of lights being turned on and off at

night, Jake suspected she slept in one of the overstuffed leather recliners in what she called the library—the room Houck had just claimed for his own. How had the agent missed that? Still, Jake wouldn't interfere. Not yet.

She ran her hands over the top half of her cane. "You haven't said who you are protecting me from."

"That's on a need-to-know basis."

"If you want me to cooperate with you, I need to know." Harmony narrowed her eyes and fastened them on Houck.

Jake watched the interplay. Finally, a glimmer of the old Harmony. She could stare down the best of them. Excluding him, although he occasionally let her win the contest of wills.

Houck blinked first. "If this gets out, it could cause a diplomatic incident."

"That's nothing new."

"It's tied to research you helped with a few years ago," Houck said.

Harmony shook her head. "Can you be any more vague? You aren't earning any points."

The agent stared at the floor. "It's a small faction with ties to a minority political group."

"Get to the point, Doan. That describes several hundred groups."

"Sweden." Houck spat out.

Sweden? What's so important about Sweden? Jake couldn't remember the last time the country had made the news.

Harmony clutched her cane to her shoulder and threw it like a spear, barely missing Doan's head. It gouged a dent in the door and clattered to the floor.

"Sweden. It had to be Sweden." Tears streamed down her cheeks.

Jake rolled off the bed and headed to the bathroom to grab the box of tissues, setting them in front of Harmony. "What's the story about Sweden?" he asked Houck.

Houck shook his head. "They only gave me an overview."

Harmony blew her nose. "It couldn't have been something from five or ten years ago. Nooo, it had to be this one."

Jake was too sore to kneel in front of her. Instead, he put his fingers under her chin, tilted her head up, and forced her to look at him. "What about Sweden, Angel?"

She sniffed and looked away. "It was a five-minute-long transmission intelligence picked up. Half was in plain English once Eli unscrambled it, the rest was encrypted. When we figured it out, it wasn't important. Just information about widely publicized troop movements. It was the last job we did together."

"I'm still lost. If it wasn't important, how can it have anything to do with what's going on now?" Jake asked, swiveling to face Houck.

"Intelligence suspects a crypto trap was built into the message, and used to identify Mr. Hennessey," Houck explained.

"Let me connect the dots here. Eli and Angel do their magic for an unnamed agency. Shortly after, Eli is killed and Angel is severely injured in an accident. Now, you suspect she's being threatened by the group she helped expose? The accident was deliberate, and Eli was murdered?"

Houck nodded. "That's the way I read it. I haven't decided if the attack on you was meant to draw Mrs. Duprie-Hennessey out of hiding or throw her emotionally off-balance and make her more vulnerable. Or both. There's no doubt that if they wanted to kill you, you'd be dead."

"Just like that," Harmony hissed. "Two years, and every day, I still cry for Eli. And just like that, you're saying everything I thought was true was a lie. Now, when I see that semitruck headed towards us, instead of the comfort of knowing Eli's death was fast, I must deal with it being deliberate. On top of that, I'm responsible for a dear old friend being attacked. How many more of my friends will get hurt before your agency gets its act together, Doan?"

"I've got connections." Jake put his hand on her shoulder. He longed to pull her into his arms, but he wasn't physically capable of it, and she wasn't ready. "I can hide you where you can't be tracked until Houck solves his security breech."

"Can you do that, Jake?" she asked.

"Fake documents are hard to get, but it can be done. You'll need to live like you don't have any money until we get you established in a new location. Do you prefer Wyoming or Oregon?"

"The agency has a series of safe houses. We'll set you both up. Separately, of course," Houck said.

Jake shook his head. "No. You might have a leak, and I need uninhibited access. I can't do what needs to be done under the watchful eye of the government."

"You'd do that for me?" Harmony whispered.

Jake considered the consequences. It would mean he'd never be able to pull another heist. She was worth it. "Before I went to prison, I asked Eli to keep an eye on you for me. He did a fine job for all those years. Now it's time for me to repay the favor and take care of you for him."

"I can't allow you to risk her life for your speculations," Houck said.

"You've got it wrong, Agent. It's not Harmony's life I'm risking, it's mine."

She nodded. "Look me in the eye, Jake."

He didn't ask questions. Or blink.

Harmony looked away first. "I'm out of practice."

"And I've gotten better."

She grinned, but didn't argue. Pressing one hand against the desktop, she rose. "Give me my cane, Doan."

What was she up to? Jake imagined the gears turning in her head, but he'd never been able to read her mind.

"Where's the safest place in Oak Grove, Jake?" she asked as she studied the rubber tip of the cane.

"The cop shop, I suppose, and with the personnel cuts the last few years, it leaves a lot to be desired. Next to that, your house. No one has removed the security features Eli added for the company."

"It was never high on the list of priorities after Eli's death, and my therapist suggested I come back and run the business from here. Thought it would be good therapy. Instead, I took my life in a different direction."

With the tip of the cane, she tapped Doan on the

shoulder. "You can take the small bedroom on the second floor. I'll convert the library into my room."

She'd caved? Jake couldn't believe it. What angle was she working?

"I'll verify with the office that the computer is updated and still runs over an encrypted connection," she continued. "I'll need access to the entire case file by tomorrow afternoon. You can do that, right?"

Houck's eyes narrowed. "Not without going through proper channels."

Harmony rolled her eyes. "We don't have time for channels. Make it happen or I will take Jake up on his offer. Remember, I have more at stake in this than you do."

And there she was. The Harmony he remembered. Jake thought about telling Houck he should listen to her, but she didn't need his help.

She continued. "How long will it take you to move your equipment from the Formby house to mine?"

A nerve twitched in Houck's cheek. "The Formby house?"

"The empty house across the street. That is you who's been up in the attic, right? If not, we have a bigger problem."

"Yes, that's me," Houck admitted. "How did you know?"

Harmony waved a hand in the air. "The Oak Grove rumor mill."

He'd started the rumor, Jake thought with satisfaction. Or did it have more than one source? He didn't have time to decide because Harmony turned her attack on him.

"And you, Jake, you've always liked the room with the big window on the third floor. You can bunk there until we get this mess straightened out."

That wouldn't happen. He couldn't trust himself to be that close to her and not take advantage of the situation. "Thanks for the offer, but like I told Houck, I have businesses to run. Besides, you need someone with their ear to the rumor mill, and there's no one in a better position for that than me."

"Doan can't protect both of us if we're in different places."

Jake reached out and touched her cheek. He longed to do more, but it wasn't the right time. "Houck's job is to protect you, not me. Now I know I'm a target, I'll be more careful. I'll move every few days. Get a room at more than one motel at a time, change my schedule. Mostly, I'll stay away from you. Got any other ideas, Houck?"

The agent rubbed his chin. "Spend as much time as you can with people you trust. That may be hard while you're recuperating, but it provides less of a vector for a second attack."

Or put more friends in harm's way. His phone vibrated in his pocket, and he moved his hand from Harmony's cheek to answer. He had to be careful and not allow himself to get sucked into caring too much for her. Again.

"It's Thomason," he said, glancing at the screen before pushing the button to answer. Without a greeting, he said, "She's here. And so is Houck. You might as well come up and join the party. Oh, and bring a chair with you."

Jake chuckled. "If you ask her nicely, she might tell us how she snuck past her bodyguards. We haven't gotten that far."

A brief pause followed as Jake listened to Thomason. "Right. We'll see you in a few."

He hung up and returned the phone to his pocket. "Darn it. I should have told him to bring some munchies and soda with him."

Chapter 8

Jake tossed on the unfamiliar hotel mattress, trying to find a comfortable position. The meds had taken the edge off the pain, but he still hurt in places he hadn't known were injured.

At least he didn't have to worry about Harmony for the night. Thomason had extracted a solemn promise from her to behave for the next twenty-four hours. That gave Houck time to move in and get her setup with access to the case files. He hoped the FASS agent wouldn't screw up his chance by hiding information from her.

Jake had started weaving his web of deception by making a reservation at the motel out by the interstate. Tomorrow, after his doctor's appointment, he'd move into the suddenly out-of-service suite across the hall while officially remaining in this room. The final touch would be taking his last remodeling venture, a two-bedroom ranch house, off the market. Sarah would understand; she hadn't received any offers for the past month. That would give him his choice of three places to hide out.

He adjusted the spare pillow under his broken arm

for added support. He still couldn't comprehend that someone would come after Harmony two years after the initial attack.

The town's sidewalks had rolled up for the night long ago; but the occasional car hissing past on the street below assured Jake he wasn't the only one still awake. He curled up on his right side, looking for a new way to lie. A couple of shots of fine whiskey might help him sleep, but he resorted to the old trick of counting backward from a hundred.

❋ ❋ ❋

"Where are we going?" Jake asked as Thomason turned right, instead of left, out of the clinic parking lot. "If you've got cop business to take care of, I can get another ride."

"I can officially claim as work anything doing with you or Harmony," Thomason grinned. "And since this concerns the both of you, I've doubled the justification."

"Let me guess. You promised Harmony you'd bring me by to see her." Jake tugged on the seatbelt to relieve the pressure on his shoulder. "Look at me. I've got more bruises showing than I did yesterday. Do you think this is a good idea?"

"She threatened to retract her promise to behave if I didn't." Thomason's mouth twitched. "Houck hasn't got her the files yet, and she's bored. I don't want her leaving the house when we have our backs turned."

"She can't go far. I'm no doctor, but after two years, therapy should have her walking better than she does."

Jake winced as they bounced over a pothole.

"Sorry about that." Thomason was more careful steering around the next bump. "It worries me, too. She won't talk to Sarah about it, either. Harmony told her the doctors have it under control."

"She needs a better doctor," Jake grumbled.

Thomason pulled the cop car into the driveway of the Victorian house, behind the black sedan with a federal license plate. "Keep your thoughts to yourself and put on a happy face."

Jake perched on the edge of the seat of an overstuffed leather chair, afraid if he sat back, he'd never get out again without help. Harmony had coerced Houck into playing butler for the visit. A soda and plate of crackers and cheese sat on the end table by his right elbow. Houck was probably responsible for the fire burning in the fireplace, too. Jake doubted Harmony had gotten on the floor to start it.

She sat in an upright padded wooden chair, with a matching plate of munchies nearby. Thomason and Houck had wandered upstairs so the agent could show off his surveillance equipment. Jake wished he could get a better look at it, too.

"So, no cast today?" she asked, pretending to sip her soda.

"The doc wants to give the swelling one more day to go down." Jake adjusted his sling. "He needs another look at my bruises and to check for any new bleeding. My pride got hurt as bad as anything else."

He waited for her to come back with a smart remark. Something about his ego needing to be taken down a peg or two. It didn't happen. Instead, she leaned forward. "What isn't Doan telling me?"

Jake rubbed a bruised spot on his cheek. "You're aware he's probably got this room bugged?"

Harmony picked up what looked like a remote control and aimed it at a panel on the wall. A red light flashed. "That takes care of that. A little upgrade of Eli's. It emits a low-level electronic buzz, too quiet for most humans to hear, and will interfere with any recording. He got tired of having to scan for listening devices."

She lowered her head, but not before Jake saw drops of water glittering on her cheeks.

"Angel," he said softly.

She sniffed. "I'll be all right. I can be doing fine, when—wham—it hits me that he's never coming back. And it's hard."

"You're allowed to miss him."

"People think I should be ready to move on, but I don't know that I'll ever be."

"That's why you're returning to Oak Grove. To get away from other people's expectations." Jake got up and put a hand on her shoulder.

Harmony laid her hand on top of his. "Promise me you'll never breathe a word of that to anyone. My therapists would have a field day with it."

"For you? I promise." He feared he'd regret that later.

"You've been a good friend." She patted his hand. "Now, what isn't Doan telling me?"

He sensed his dismissal and returned to his chair. "My

guess is that when you finally see the documents, they'll be full of retractions and erasures done so well that you won't know they're missing. And I'm not the expert at spotting them."

"That was Eli's job." Harmony held up her hand. "Don't worry, the tears will wait. I've got my business face on."

"Can anyone from the company help?"

She shook her head. "No one has that level of security clearance. I won't put the reputation of Shifter Technologies at risk."

"Good. I need my investment protected." Jake smiled as much as he could. His face still hurt.

Her eyes widened. "What?"

Shit. She didn't know. "Eli left me a small portion of the profits from the company yearly. Not a share, the allowance depends on how well the company does. When I die, the provision ends."

"No one told me. There were lots of details the lawyers dealt with. I just had to sign off on the overall paperwork. Not that I wanted to deal with any of it." Harmony stared at the fire.

Jake sat silent, allowing her time to absorb the new information. She picked up the little remote and aimed it at the panel.

"I don't know how long I'll get away with using that before Doan figures out that there's a flaw in his technology." A sliver of a grin crossed her face. "I always enjoyed getting one over on law enforcement. I learned that from you."

He cocked his head. "You were a natural."

Footsteps on the stair ended the conversation. Harmony picked up her glass of soda and stared at the fire until Thomason and Houck entered the room. Then, as smoothly as if all they'd done was discuss the weather, she asked, "What do you say, Freddie? Does Houck's setup look good to you?"

"So, what did you really think of Houck's equipment?" Jake asked Thomason on the way back to the hotel. As far as the cop knew, that's where Jake was spending the night.

"It's impressive, but it can't replace live bodies." As they idled at a red light, Thomason checked the computer display on his dash.

"Something wrong?" Jake asked.

"It's probably someone looking for an unfamiliar address." Thomason looked in his review mirror. "They flipped a U-turn and came back around to get behind us. Bad maneuver to execute in view of a cop."

"Unless they deliberately tried to draw your attention, to distract you from something else." Jake leaned forward to get a different view out of the side mirror.

As the light turned green, Thomason punched a few buttons on his dash before continuing down the street. "Backup will be here in a few. That'll give me time to assess the situation. Hang on. I'm going to take a right."

The turn signal of the police vehicle automatically started when Thomason dialed in the change of lanes. Jake had disabled that feature on his car, along with a few others. He'd never have the control he did with older models, but the changes gave him the semblance of greater autonomy.

Two blocks down the road, Thomason made a second right, then checked his computer display. "Still with us. I'd offer to drop you off at the coffee shop a block ahead, but I can't guarantee your safety."

"It's hard to guess which of us is the target." Jake rubbed his chin. "It would be interesting to have a conversation with whomever is in that car."

"I've got no probable cause to stop it unless it develops a mechanical or electronic issue. You never know with these modern cars." Thomason glanced at Jake and chuckled.

Jake checked his mirror again. "Isn't the right headlight out, Detective Thomason?"

"It appears to have a loose wire, Mr. Hennessey. I think I should radio it in before it creates a hazard."

"How lucky that one of your fellow officers has just pulled onto the street behind him."

Red and blue lights lit the cars. Thomason braked to slow the following vehicle. Things were going by the book. Until they didn't.

The black four-door sedan rammed into the left corner of the rear bumper of Thomason's car, shoving it into the curb, and then sped away. The collision thrust Jake forward, his seatbelt cutting into his shoulder. Pain radiated through his entire upper body, and he bit his lip to hold back a scream.

Thomason killed the engine and unfastened his seat belt as the second police car gave chase. "You okay?"

"No air bags?" Jake asked through gritted teeth.

"Law enforcement vehicles are exempt from the

regulations. They were proven to interfere with police duties. With a special code, I could have overridden the command to shut down the engine, but I didn't think you were up to taking part in the pursuit."

Jake hunched his shoulders. "It's not on the list of doctor-approved activities."

"I'll get you a new driver to take you back to the hotel." Thomason's fingers bounced against the keyboard. "I'll be tied up with reports. Chief Santos will yell about the overtime, but he'll have to find the money in the budget somewhere."

"Did you get a look at the driver?"

The detective shook his head. "Not enough to be useful. No worries, the in-car cameras will take care of that. I'll come by later to share the results."

❀ ❀ ❀

"Let me guess. State police found the car north of town and it was stolen." Jake unwrapped the sandwich Thomason had brought him. Not only had he had time for a long, hot bath while waiting, he'd caught a nap, and now he was hungry.

Thomason nodded. "If that's not bad enough, the on-board system didn't pick up the license information, either the physical or digital display. I've heard about devices with a masking capability, but they didn't find one on the vehicle."

They were having the discussion in Jake's original hotel room. If Thomason was being tracked, Jake didn't want his exact location revealed.

"So, they've taken the technology portable. It was bound to happen." Jake wondered how much it cost on the black market.

"I remember when I could maintain my car. Now cars are all electronic." One side of Thomason's mouth rose. "I feel like a dinosaur."

"Whatever happened to your old Mustang?" Jake asked before taking a bite.

"I finally gave up and sold it to a museum. I couldn't keep it road-legal anymore. How about your Charger?"

Even four days ago, Jake couldn't have imagined having this conversation with any member of law enforcement. "It's in storage. I maintain a license that allows me to display it in parades and such. I think it's been six months since the last time I fired it up. The cost of gas is ridiculous."

"If you take it for a spin, I'd like to hitch a ride. After you recuperate, of course. Speaking of which, do you plan to stay here?"

"Define 'here'." Jake grinned. "It'll be like playing whack-a-mole to find me."

"The question is—who is trying to find you?"

"My question is why? Is it really Harmony they are after? Or is it me, and they are using the rumors about Harmony as a cover? Because what today proved is they don't want me dead. I have no clue what they do want."

Chapter 9

Jake rubbed his nose, holding back a sneeze. His heavily bandaged arm made everything more difficult, but he was determined to get out of the hotel without being seen. He'd navigated the dusty crawl spaces for the utilities before, but never with a fractured arm. He'd removed his sling to make it easier. At least he didn't have to drag a broken leg through the tight quarters.

Jake suspected someone on the force was sabotaging Thomason. Freezing him out of important information; giving him bad assignments; and, of course, involving him in a hit-and-run. So, Jake's immediate goal was the black-market scanner—stashed in a secret partition in his apartment—that picked up not only old-fashioned police radios, but the Wi-Fi of the on-board police computers.

The crawl way exited into housekeeping closet next to a set of unused stairs. Jake stood and stretched, groaning softly as sore muscles protested. After checking the hallway was empty, he slipped into the stairwell and down the steps. When he reached the first floor, he checked his watch, and waited until exactly 10 p.m., when

Webb was scheduled to turn off the security cameras. At the other end of the hallway, a green light flashed on the closest device. At 10:05 pm, it still flashed. Had Webb forgotten? At 10:07 pm, it turned red, and Jake dashed down the hall to the empty delivery dock of the hotel. From there, the rental car was a quick jog through the alley to employee parking, courtesy of Webb.

If his unknown opponents were smart, they'd be keeping surveillance on his apartment. Jake hoped they'd underestimated him.

❋ ❋ ❋

The rake leaning against the back gate was Jake's first assurance that everything remained secure at the run-down house he called home. His apartment was three small rooms but all that he needed. He had little traps all the way to the top of the back porch stairs. The pile of leaves, the metal bucket filled with dirty water, the loose rocks scattered on the sidewalk. The final guarantee was Lonnie's dog, Bob, fast asleep on the torn welcome mat.

Those were his poor man's measures. His aim was to outfit the apartment's door with an almost-new electronic alarm programmed to feed information directly to a modified watch. He planned to attach a second sensor to his bedroom window.

A handful of bacon treats kept Bob, a bulldog, happy while Jake disappeared into his closet and gathered his tools. It wouldn't be the first time Bob had kept him company while he worked. That was when he tackled a project for the bar. Never for anything as important as this.

A few years back, Jake had helped his landlord, Lonnie, with repairs on the old home where Jake rented most of the second floor. On the sly, he'd added a phony wall in the attic, using wood salvaged from a demolished house, making it appear to be part of the original build. The only access to the partition was by the ladder behind a false panel in his closet. The space gave him enough room to store a few items of dubious legality and, if it came down to it, himself. He didn't know if he'd be able to get Harmony up there.

With Lonnie downstairs, snoring in front of the TV, and the second upstairs apartment empty, Jake didn't have to worry about the noise from his drill. The design of the handle made it steady enough for him to operate one-handed.

Similar to alarms that operated on the principal of a continuous beam of light, the alert worked on magnetism and with power supplied by hearing aid batteries. It sent a signal to Jake's watch over the internet. The system wasn't flawless. If his internet went down, so did his security. It was good enough for now.

Jake sent Bob out into the backyard for one more trip before the dog settled in for the night. There was more work to do once Jake got back to the hotel, but he had another stop to make first.

"Hey, Eddie," Jake said, as a group of kids wearing Penn State jackets headed out the door. He'd skulked in a back corner of the convenience store until they were gone.

"Hennessey!" Eddie looked up from the counter and whistled. "Well, damn. I heard you were in rough shape, but this…"

Jake shrugged. "At least I'm not dead."

"Yeah, there were a few rumors about that, but I figured you had a trick or two up your sleeve. Or should I say, up your cast?" She looked dubiously at his arm.

"The cast is supposed to go on tomorrow. This is temporary." He piled an assortment of snacks on the counter.

"Thank heavens it's not your leg. You can still make a quick getaway," she smirked.

He couldn't, but he didn't share that information. "So, how do the rumors spin this?"

"People are asking who you were cheating on. But you haven't been serious about anyone in forever. Not that some of us ladies wouldn't mind giving you a shot at stealing our hearts."

Jake put his hand to his chest. "I'll never be able to decide on just one woman."

"It's your lucky day. We can share. I'll take Monday, Betty can have Tuesday, Mary can schedule you in on Wednesdays." Eddie waggled her eyebrows and laughed.

It hurt too much to laugh, but Jake couldn't help himself. He leaned against the counter and clutched his side. "You're a cruel woman, Eddie."

"You don't laugh enough, Hennessey. So, I do what I can." She wiped the corners of her eyes.

"And I appreciate everything," he answered.

The front door of the store opened, and a middle-aged couple entered. Eddie winked. "Is there anything else I can help you with, sir?"

Jake reached over and snagged two bags of pretzels to add to his stack. "That should do it."

At eleven p.m., they locked the doors of The Towers for security, and the only way to get in was to have the front desk clerk buzz open the door. Except for employees. And Jake. He recognized the undercover police car parked across the street, so he played by the rules, and waited for Anton, the night clerk, to unlock the door.

"You've got a watchdog tonight," Jake said as Anton—a tall, dark-skinned man—shut the door behind them.

"Two of them are taking turns." Anton grinned. "The word is you're responsible. It'll help me stay awake tonight. Do you need help carrying your things to your room?"

Jake didn't want Anton to know which room he was staying in. Or the weight of the second bag. "I'm good. There are pretzels in the front bag. I seem to remember you liking them. You quit smoking, right?"

Anton rolled his eyes and retrieved the offered snacks. "I'm trying. These should help. Have a good night, Mr. Hennessey."

It would be a good night if he could zero in on the frequencies the police scanner needed, Jake thought. With two patrols trading off duties, it would make things easier. There'd be lots of radio chatter to scan. Well, more than normal for Oak Grove.

"That's a 10-11, not a 10-14," the app on Jake's phone crackled.

He grinned. Radar, old Mr. McReady's German Shepherd, must have gotten out again. The dog was known to peek in the windows of the neighborhood when he had a chance, causing prowler reports. That, and Mr. McCready out wandering, trying to find the pooch. That call wouldn't end up generating a need for encrypted communications like he hoped to track.

"Standard doggy treats did the trick, and he's home now. I'm heading back."

"10-4. Don't forget to drive by The Towers." That was Donna, who had been the dispatcher for as long as Jake could remember.

"Who's on duty?"

There was a quick beep, and the app went quiet. They'd switched to the silent mode, and the chance Jake had been waiting for. He'd already tried twice to determine the local channel with no luck. Perhaps the third time would be the charm.

The hacker who had created the device hadn't had time to give Jake much advice. Of course, they'd been busy with other activities. There were several "standard" bandwidths, but departments were advised not to use them, and instead to hire a specialist to set up the system. Jake was betting on the city going cheap and not doing that.

He punched the third batch of numbers into the

device. The box emitted a mechanical hum, but his phone didn't react.

Through the cracks in the curtains, he watched a police vehicle pull alongside the undercover car. Maybe that's what happened. They were going to continue their conversation face to face. No telling how long that would last.

Jake yawned. He'd been warned it was a finicky process and to not expect a miracle. He'd call it a night—no, morning—and try again later.

❊ ❊ ❊

"The swelling has gone down nicely. As long as you behave yourself, the cast will do its job and I won't need to see you for another week." Doc Gabe held Jake's face between his hands and scrutinized the scabs and bruising. "Are the pain meds working? Or is it stress? You look as if you aren't getting enough sleep."

"Finding a comfortable position is hard," Jake explained. He was avoiding taking the pills because he needed to be aware of his surroundings.

"Pillows. Lots of them. Ask Trina for a brochure on your way out. Elevating your arm will help with the pain, too. Have the police found your attacker?" the doctor asked as he washed his hands.

"Not yet." Jake slipped on the oversized shirt he'd bought. "Have you heard any rumors?"

"Not a single one. And that's not normal. If they received any medical care, it wasn't here. What have you got yourself mixed up with?"

Another dead end. Jake was used to making his own luck, but his usual good fortune had abandoned him. "I don't know, but I need to figure it out."

"Or let Freddie do his job." Trina said, coming into the exam room. "He's here, by the way. And pissed off you didn't call him for a ride."

Jake could handle Thomason. "He's a busy man. I didn't want to bother him."

"Right. I believe that excuse. Doc, you've got a patient waiting in room five. I'll finish up in here."

Jake started to slide off the bed, and she shook her head. Once. It was enough for him to get the message, and he stayed where he was until Doc Gabe had left.

"What did I do wrong?" he asked.

"Not you. Me and some of the staff were discussing your case and how fishy it is." She wiped down the mobile table, cleaning up bits of plaster.

"I won't disagree. What makes you think so?"

"Cops. Little things they say when they don't know we're listening."

Jake arched an eyebrow. "You've got my attention."

"The old timers remember when Chief Sorenson started. One thing he did was get rid of a few bad apples. Probably before you came to town. Anyway, everyone mostly trusted the cops. Now, not so much." She still refused to look him in the eye.

"I'm aware of the rumors. Santos seems to be square."

Trina closed the door. "Those new guys he brought in are all about law and order to the max. They're so busy trying to impress Santos that they ignore community policing and make it their mission to elevate their stats.

Suspects come in with more injuries than are justified by the crimes they're accused of. Nothing that can be proven, but the nods and glances are there. Even if the suspects get off, they've already been punished. There are mutters about folks wanting to leave, but having no money to get out of town."

"That's bad, but what does it have to do with me?" Jake had his own suspicions, but he wanted to see what Trina and her coworkers thought.

She snorted. "Don't play naive. If they could catch you doing something illegal, what a score that would be. Your reputation, deserved or not, makes you a target."

"I agree with the idea, but what has changed?"

"Jenny has a theory. You probably haven't met her, she moved to town a few months ago to take care of her grandmother. Anyway, one of the new cops—she thinks it was Officer Morrison, but isn't sure—was upset because Freddie interfered with a bust he was trying to make. And there you have a double whammy—get revenge on Freddie and get rid of you."

"It's farfetched enough to be plausible." Jake frowned. "Thomason is such a straight-arrow he won't believe it. I certainly can't take the suspicions to Santos."

Trina handed Jake his discharge papers. "As long as you know you can't trust everyone."

Chapter 10

Jake leaned his hip against the front desk of the medical clinic. Thomason was at the front door, talking on the phone. "How's it going, Belinda?"

The clinic receptionist looked up from the computer screen and her lips curled into a smile. She flicked a lock of dark hair away from her face and tilted back in her chair. "Jake! I heard you got yourself into a spot of trouble. I've been out of town and missed the excitement. Are you the reason a cop is cluttering my lobby?"

"I'm afraid so. He believes he has to protect me. All I really need is for you to comfort me." He smirked. "Wouldn't be the first time."

They'd hung out together once a long time ago, after Belinda had broken up with her boyfriend. It hadn't been an official date, but they'd both had a good time that lasted the entire night. Then she'd gotten back together with her boyfriend, now fiancé. That didn't stop Jake from flirting with her, and her flirting back at every opportunity.

"I could sneak you out the back door while Thomason

is busy." She jerked her head towards the rear.

Jake gave an exaggerated sigh. "While that sounds like fun, I am trying to cooperate. So, I'll pass for now."

"That's a shame." She giggled. "It's time for me to go on my break. And here comes Thomason."

She pulled a piece of paper from the printer and handed it to Jake. "Don't forget, you have an appointment next week. See you then."

He blew her a kiss, then turned as the detective approached the desk. "Thomason! I didn't plan to interfere with your day. If you have business to handle, I'll find another ride. I need to make a stop by the bar, anyway."

"Is that allowed by doctor's orders?" Thomason raised an eyebrow.

"I'm cleared to resume normal activities as I feel up to them. Except for the arm, of course."

Thomason glanced at Belinda.

She consulted the computer. "That is correct, Detective. Mr. Hennessey has remarkable powers of recovery."

Jake hid his grin. She'd had no complaints in that department.

"It's been a long time since I've been to your bar, Hennessey," Thomason said as they walked to his patrol car.

"No offense, but I prefer it that way." He was in the middle of sending Danny a text telling him to get the customers with warrants to leave. "The Purple Onion isn't exactly a cop-friendly place."

Thomason opened the front passenger-side door for him. "I've checked the records. It's clean, except for a few noise complaints. And Stella Murcat has a beef with the smoke that drifts into her apartment from the back entrance." He shut the door firmly, walked around to the driver's side, and climbed in.

"We've done everything we can to stop that. Put up barriers and fans, but she's not happy." Jake shrugged his good shoulder. "Her real problem is that my customers smoke at all."

Thomason started the engine and pulled out of the parking lot. "I know that, but some people believe you have a contact with city council or the force covering for you."

"There are people who say you are that person," Jake said quietly.

"I'm aware of that. However, I won't allow those suspicions to get in the way of doing my job." His lips forming a taut line, Thomason glanced in his review mirror and signaled for the left turn to get to the wrong side of town.

"You've always treated me fairly, and I don't like the idea of interfering with your career. You should foist me off on some rookie."

"That's not my call. Besides, no one knows your history like I do. The good and the bad. And you're the one who came to me when you discovered an issue with Harmony."

"It comes down to Harmony, doesn't it?" Jake rubbed the back of his head.

Thomason pulled into a spot in front of the bar.

"We're on the same side when it comes to her. How many times have you risked your life for her?"

Jake stared out the windshield. "More times than she—or anyone—will ever realize. And I'll do it again if I have to."

No surprise, the bar only had four customers when Jake and Thomason strolled in, and none of them were in any current legal trouble, to the best of Jake's knowledge. Danny was stacking clean glasses, trying to look busy while Rene scrubbed the floor in the back corner.

A wooden chair scraped against the floor. "God damn it," Jorge said, half-standing and staring at Jake. "Gossip said it was bad, but we didn't expect this."

"Yeah, well, I'm a tough one to kill." Jake held out his hand. "It's good to see you."

That was as much of a reaction as he'd get, at least in public. If any of them had any information to share, they would have told Danny or Rene.

Jake honestly had paperwork to do over the secure line he'd had installed. Not as reinforced as Houck's connection, but it would discourage all but the most determined hackers. His hacker friend had verified it in exchange for a hard-to-acquire bottle of old Scotch. He took pity on Thomason, who appeared uncomfortable sitting in the open bar, and invited him to the office for a cup of coffee.

"Do you trust your customers?" Thomason asked, setting his cup on Jake's desk.

Jake looked up from the computer screen. "No, but most of them don't have the motivation to get involved with anything that takes effort. I can't imagine that any of them are connected to the attack."

"I'm frustrated." The detective frowned. "All my normal sources have dried up."

"Or someone threatened them," Jake suggested, tapping at the computer screen.

"I've considered that, but they seem as puzzled as anyone else. Which leads me back to an outsider, and leaves us dependent on Houck."

Jake nodded. "Has he given Harmony access to the files yet?"

"I don't know." Thomason rotated his cup without taking a drink. "I was tied up at the office with a last-minute report and didn't have a chance to visit her. Why Santos put it off is beyond me."

"Poor management? Or to keep you away from Angel or me?"

With a smirk, the detective said, "He's been trying to impress the city council with his monthly reports since he took over for Sorenson. No one can replicate Sorenson's magic."

Jake chuckled. "Angel did those reports for him. I don't know when she started, but she kept it up until he retired. I only found out because Eli let it slip."

"That explains a lot." Thomason shook his head and grinned. "I suspected the two of them were keeping a secret, but it was none of my business."

Jake took a last look at the liquor order and hit the button to send it to his supplier. One task down. He wanted to celebrate with a shot of whiskey, but his watchdog would get upset with him for disobeying doctor's orders, so he settled for a swallow of coffee. He needed to do payroll, anyway.

"Shit. What are the chances that she was doing other favors for him?" Thomason put his cup on the desk and stood, walking back and forth across the small space. "There were times he'd come up with leads the rest of us didn't think of. I always figured it was his experience that let him do that."

Jake hadn't guessed the detective was a pacer. He always seemed so in control. "Will she own up to it?"

"How do I convince her that someone found out about her involvement and this unknown person has carried a grudge all these years?"

"It sounds rather improbable."

Thomason rolled his eyes. "This is Harmony we're talking about. Things have a way of happening when she's involved."

The honey-whiskey slid smoothly down Jake's throat. After securing Jake's promise to not stay at work too long, Thomason had taken off to talk to Harmony. Which gave Jake a few precious minutes alone.

He mused over the discussion. The lady had more depth to her than he'd realized. It was a reminder that she was far out of his league. But he needed to protect her. Somehow.

The security camera feed alerted him to the fact that Danny was on his way back, and he finished the rest of his drink and moved the glass to the shelf behind him. Danny acted like a nanny sometimes—he thought Jake drank too much—and Jake wasn't in the mood to listen to his "suggestions". He had the payroll program up on the screen before Danny made it to the office door.

Danny knocked, but didn't wait for Jake's response before entering. That was their standard way of operating.

"If we get too many visits like that, it'll cut into your customer base." Danny settled into the chair across the desk without asking.

"Then I'll have to hire some cute wait staff to bring in the college crowd." Jake grinned. They'd jokingly had this discussion before.

Danny laughed. "As long as you don't make me wear a sexy outfit."

"You want pink, or white with blue fringes?"

"Please, Lord, no fringes." Danny raised his face and looked towards the ceiling. "Anything but fringes."

"Honestly? I suspect there's more going on than he's sharing. Have you heard anything over the past few days you couldn't tell me on the phone?"

"The only thing anyone talked about was the attack. Now that you've shown your face in public, as ugly as it is, that may change."

Jake nodded. "As long as I'm forced to hang out with Thomason, folks will be reluctant to talk to me. That's where you step in. I'll spend most of my time elsewhere, and you run the place."

"Business as usual." Danny grinned.

"And that's why I pay you the big bucks."

Jake depended on Danny too much, but the envelope of cash he'd slipped to his long-time employee should help ease the pain, at least until Jake was more mobile. Danny took Jake to his apartment so he could collect a suitcase of clothes and check that his security system was intact. Then, a ride share took Jake to his house for sale, with a bonus for the driver to take an envelope to Webb at the hotel. The tactic should confuse anyone following from a distance.

The house had enough furniture installed for staging that Jake could take a nap. Both water and electric were on, a point that helped make sales. Which meant he could take a long soak in the spa tub in the remodeled bathroom first.

A black bag covered the for-sale sign, so Sarah had honored his wishes to take it off the market. With the doors locked, he didn't have to worry about interruptions. He stretched out in the two-person garden tub with the water as hot as he could stand it; the jets bubbling away, and Cherry Lee—his favorite singer, a woman who specialized in old-fashioned torch songs—crooning from his watch, and closed his eyes. Even half-asleep, he alerted to the beeps of the electronic front door lock being opened.

He reached for his towel, preferring not to be completely naked if he was about to be murdered. Then he relaxed as he recognized the voices of two women coming from the front room. "Can't pass up on an opportunity to make a sale, Sarah?"

"Jake?" she called.

"I'm testing out the spa. Feel free to show Harmony around. I'm not fit for company." He opted not to change that. They had intruded on him. Besides, he wasn't ashamed of his body. He'd stayed in good shape. Except for the broken arm and assorted cuts and bruises. And the many scars he'd earned along the way.

"I apologize. I didn't know you were here. Harmony wanted to see this place before we started a full-scale house hunt." Sarah's voice came from the end of the hall.

"That was the idea, that I'd be in hiding. Go ahead and check out the place while you're here. I can assure you the contractor does quality work, and would add any finishing touches the client wants, if a price can be agreed on. It doesn't have the loftiness of a Victorian, but the Cape Cod styling has been given a modern touch. Personally, I consider the selling point is the master bath—it has a combination of features you won't find in many homes in Oak Grove, especially at the special price the contractor will discount for you." He had intended to take advantage of the steam shower himself, after the spa water cooled.

"Let's go see the kitchen," Sarah said.

So much for his leisurely session. He couldn't relax, knowing they were just around the corner. He got out, dried off, got dressed, and joined the women in the kitchen. They were examining the various shelves and drawers.

"I didn't install a spice cabinet," he said. "I don't

know how much of an incentive for a sale that would give the new homeowner. What do you think, Angel? And where is your watchdog?"

"Doan and Freddie are out in the car, arguing with the special agent in charge of the case. I'm not sure about what. They refused to tell me." Harmony turned and ran her eyes from his head to his feet.

At least his clothes hid the worst of the bruises, like the boot mark in the middle of his chest. There wasn't a way to fix the discoloration on his face. "They shouldn't have let you come in without checking out the house first."

"That was my fault," Sarah interrupted. "I told Freddie about the security system and that if the alarm went off, you would call 9-1-1."

She was right. "Don't do it again, Sarah."

"Back off, Jake." Sarah poked him in the chest–gently–with one finger. "Harmony has the right to live her life. She can't stay cooped up in that house forever. And what gives? I thought you were on her side."

Chapter 11

Jake studied the kitchen stove, wondering if it needed to be leveled. He liked everything in his houses as perfect as possible for potential buyers. "What do you expect? I'm looking out for Harmony's safety," he told Sarah.

Harmony had been inspecting a cupboard, and she slammed the door of the cupboard closed. "Who are you protecting me from? I'm about to reach out to old friends and ask them to yank Doan off the case."

"Do it." Jake leaned against the sink. "Put the word out. Get your connections involved. The more the merrier. You have nothing to hide."

"I'd hurt Doan's feelings." She took an audible breath and lowered her gaze. "And Freddie's."

"Houck came into town with a chip on his shoulder. And he lied to you for six months, so why do you care? Now, Thomason deserves more consideration." Jake glanced through the front window. "And they are on their way in, so make your decision."

The door opened before she responded.

"Hennessey!" Houck barked, drawing his revolver.

"What are you doing here?"

"Calm down, Special Agent," Sarah said. "Jake owns this place. We're intruding on him."

"Technically, it belongs to my construction firm." Jake kept his good hand where Houck could see it. "It's more of a hobby. I only tackle one or two projects a year. Didn't your research identify that?"

"Lower your weapon, Doan. I knew Jake owned this house. That's why I agreed to let Sarah bring Harmony here." Thomason crossed his arms and looked around. "Nice job, Jake. I was here several times when the place was rented out before you bought it."

Houck holstered his revolver but continued to glare at Jake.

Jake nodded. "Yeah, they were a fun bunch. I banned them from the bar. It was even more satisfying to evict them."

"Didn't I hear they were dealing drugs?" Sarah asked.

"They tried. It didn't go so well. Why they imagined they could set up shop in The Purple Onion is beyond me."

"You pop up too often," Houck said. "It makes me suspicious."

"It should." Jake raised an eyebrow. "But you approached me first. And I'm the one Harmony keeps seeking out."

"That's enough," Harmony hissed, jabbing her cane at Houck and Jake in turn. "Neither of you is king of the hill."

She quickly turned around. "And that goes for you too, Freddie."

The twirl threw her off balance, and she stumbled. Jake was the closest and grabbed her before she fell.

"Are you okay, Angel?" Jake looked over her head and exchanged a worried glance with Freddie. "Does this happen often?"

Jake couldn't resist. He held her close, longer than needed, while she regained her footing.

Her cheeks flushed. She leaned on her cane and shoved herself away. Jake let her go.

"It could happen to anybody," Harmony ran a hand through her hair. "No big deal."

Maybe she was kidding herself, but she wasn't fooling him. "I could install cork floor tiles by the stove and the sink. Less of a trip hazard than rugs," Jake said.

"I haven't seen the whole place and you're acting like I'm going to live here? Pushy, much?" The grin on her face made a lie out of her words.

Sarah giggled. "That's why he isn't allowed to come to showings. Jake gets these last-minute ideas and talks himself out of what little profit margin he's making in the first place."

"Like I said, it's more of a hobby than anything." *And a way to launder the occasional windfall.* The attention made Jake uncomfortable. "What other houses were you planning to show Harmony?"

"We discussed that newer ranch-style over on Fourth. And the two-story place in the middle of the 500 block of Willow." Sarah rubbed her chin. "I'm worried about the way the neighborhood is changing over there. What do you think, Freddie?"

Thomason shook his head. "Honestly, I'd take that one off your list."

As they discussed the recent string of thefts in that part of town, it gave Jake the opportunity to step back and expertly fade into the background. He needed to go repack his bag. The house would no longer be useful as a hideout. Not if someone had tracked Harmony here.

He left the bag on the bed and headed outside through the double doors to the little patio. It had enough room for two chairs and a small table, so the house's owner could sit and enjoy the sunrise while drinking their morning coffee.

The cozy space shrunk the moment Houck appeared around the corner from the front of the house. "Leaving?"

Jake took a deep breath, hoping for patience. "If I wanted to leave, I'd be gone. It was getting crowded inside."

Houck blinked. "Seemed like plenty of room to me."

"Too many egos."

"Point taken."

Jake wondered if Houck was one of those people who talked to fill in silence. Now was as good of a time as any to find out. He leaned against the house and closed his eyes.

"Can you talk Mrs. Duprie-Hennessey into leaving town?" Houck asked.

Jake popped one eye open. "What?"

"I'd like to get her back to Orlando. She'll be safer there. Plus, she can get better medical care."

The other eye opened. "Better than what? Pittsburgh

is just down the road. Some of the finest doctors in the nation, or so I hear."

Houck turned his back to Jake. "Or do you want her here for other reasons? Is she the target of your next scam?"

Was the agent deliberately trying to provoke him?

"Harmony is too smart to be taken in by a scam," Jake allowed a smile to crease his face. "I thought you would have figured that out after working with her for six months."

When Houck turned around, his face was flushed, and his knuckles were white. Jake pushed back the surge of satisfaction. Getting under Houck's skin felt like a win, but he still had to pretend to play by the rules. The next move was Houck's.

Thomason showed up at the door to the patio. "The ladies are ready to leave. I convinced them to go back to Harmony's house. Do you need a ride somewhere, Jake?"

"I don't think Special Agent Houck wants to be seen with me right now." Jake cocked his head in Houck's direction. "He decided I'm one of the bad guys and that I'm planning to take advantage of Harmony. Apparently, he's been using his time and resources to dig into my background instead of finding out if there's a genuine threat to her."

Thomason crossed his arms. "Use your common sense, Doan. Jake's the one who was attacked."

"Look at his record," Houck snapped.

"I've seen it. Numerous times." Thomason sighed. "He's only got one conviction. A bust I made. That was from what, thirty years ago? He did his time. There've been lots of allegations, but nothing has stuck. I've lost count of how many federal agencies have tried and failed to bring charges. Now, get over it. If you can't handle this as a professional, I'll reach out to my contacts and ask if you can be replaced."

"Mrs. Duprie-Hennessey might have something to say about that."

"About what?" Harmony asked from behind Thomason.

"Placing additional equipment in the Formby place for a new angle of coverage," Thomason said, with no hesitation. "Houck doesn't want to upset you."

She shrugged. "It's not like I have any privacy now. I'll defer to the experts. Jake, I wanted to say what a great job you did on this house. I'm nowhere near ready to buy, but it made for a nice diversion. I'm allowed so few of them."

A compliment to him and a subtle insult to Houck in one swoop. Jake's mouth wiggled as he tried to hide his smile. The lady was sharp. It was good to see her back in action. "When do you start at the library?"

"Janine is waiting for the Board of Directors' final approval. Some things never change." She clutched the door frame and stepped onto the patio. "This needs flower boxes along the front."

"Or hanging pot stands." Jake eyed the same car going down the street for the second time in the last few minutes. He didn't know every car in Oak Grove, but this one looked familiar. It didn't belong to any of his regulars, and something about it made the back of his neck tingle. In his peripheral vision, he caught Thomason rubbing his neck.

Thomason pulled his phone out of his pocket and stared at the screen, then punched a few buttons. "I've got to get back to the station. You have someone to call for a ride, Jake?"

"I need to make sure everything is locked up and I don't want to delay you." Jake would have liked for Thomason to stick around because his nerves were stretched hair-thin, but he didn't want to prevent Harmony from leaving. Call it instinct. He wanted her out of the house and back to safety.

"Gotcha. Houck, you ride with Sarah and Harmony back to the house. I'll stay with Jake." Thomason rubbed his neck again. "It'll only take a few minutes, right?"

So, the detective was feeling it too, Jake decided— whatever "it" was. And neither of them wanted to let Harmony in on the worry.

"I want to go by the library and take out a few books," Harmony said, "since Doan still hasn't gotten me access to the files I requested."

Jake raised an eyebrow. "Just how far up the chain of command is the hold-up?"

"Way above my pay grade." Houck said.

Her lips drew taut, and she closed her eyes. "Then I'll figure out a way around them."

Jake's attention was drawn to the black two-door car cruising by. The same one. For the third time. This time, the window was rolled down, and an arm hung out of it. Something glittered in the sunshine. "Thomason."

"Inside, Harmony, NOW!" The detective didn't

give her a choice. He pushed against her shoulders and shoved her inside. Her cane clattered to the ground.

Houck stood frozen, his back to the traffic. It was too late for words. Jake wasn't as fast as he used to be, but he had to be fast enough. He threw himself at the agent.

Chapter 12

Jake leaned against the refrigerator, wishing he was invisible. Being in close quarters with five cops wasn't his idea of a good time. They seemed to take up the entire front room as they were in and out, searching for evidence and conferring with each other. Houck and Thomason had been joined by three of Oak Grove's finest. Jake knew two of them—Sergeant Holt and Detective Ayres—but Officer Bellevue was a rookie..

No one had gotten hurt, but Harmony had taken a hard fall, and the bullet had grazed Jake's cast. That meant another trip to the clinic. The paramedics had left a minimum of garbage behind—the wrapper from a blood pressure cuff had gotten kicked under the kitchen table, and Jake didn't want to lean over to pick it up and draw attention to himself. He'd have to get his cleaning service in to bring the house back to its spotless condition.

Houck hadn't come out of the incident entirely unscathed. Jake's cast had rammed into his solar plexus when they hit the ground, knocking the breath out of the agent. Not on purpose, but in hindsight, Jake wished he'd thought of it.

Both Houck and Thomason had reviewed the footage from the security camera over the front door, without finding any useful information. The angle was wrong to pick up the black car's plate, and the recent Altitude was a popular model, with thousands on the road. Jake knew of three of them in town. This one could be sitting in a garage a few blocks away or be on the road to Pittsburgh. There were no identifying marks to make it stand out from every other black Altitude.

Harmony limped her way through the gauntlet of law enforcement to stand in front of him. She and Sarah had been in the guest bedroom. "Are you okay? You're awfully quiet."

He'd be better with a couple of shots of fine whiskey to soothe his nerves. "I'm trying to hear what isn't being said. And getting nowhere."

"You used to be a genius at reading body language. You've lost your touch."

"I haven't." Jake arched an eyebrow. "They are out of ideas. Nothing fits together. Except me."

Harmony leaned against the counter next to him, close enough that her floral perfume surrounded him. "And me?"

He'd been hoping to avoid that conversation. "And you. Houck wants to force you to go back to Florida if he can't get you to agree to go into hiding."

"Is that what he and Freddie were arguing about?"

"Partly. Then they took their discussion outside."

"It wouldn't do any good for me to go back to Florida."

Harmony crossed her arms and stared vacantly at the floor. "Whoever is responsible will just follow me and attack my friends there."

"Or not." Jake jerked his head towards the cops, deep in their own hushed discussion. "Because unless you have a tracker installed on you, how would anyone know you were here? Me, on the other hand… logical for someone to take a chance on me being here."

Houck broke away from the huddle. "Are you ready to go home, Mrs. Duprie? I'll take you, Thomason will accompany his wife, and the officers will go with Hennessey to the clinic."

Jake sensed Harmony stiffen beside him.

"You mean back to the Aldridge house?" she asked. "I guess I've had enough excitement for one day. Where did my cane get to?"

"You can lean on me." Jake extended his uninjured arm.

She patted it. "Thank you, but I don't want to put any extra stress on you."

The blind leading the blind. At least his condition was temporary.

"I believe your cane is in the master bedroom, ma'am," Officer Bellevue said. "I'll go check."

"Ma'am," Harmony huffed. "I swear I'll never get used to that."

Jake faked a yawn to camouflage his grin, although he sympathized with her reaction. The first time he'd been called "sir" by one of his customers had been a shock. He didn't hear it often, but he no longer cringed at the rare instances.

The young officer returned after a quick moment. "Right where I remembered," she said. "Is this old or a replica? It reminds me of one my grandpa used."

"It was a gift. I checked, and the ivory is artificial."

Bellevue swung the cane back and forth, seemingly reluctant to return the cane to Harmony. "It seems to be out of balance. My gramps had the same issue with his. Do you mind if I check the connections?"

"Mrs. Duprie can do that when we get back to the house," Houck interrupted.

"No, let her." Harmony limped a few steps closer. "Show me how."

Surely Harmony was smart enough to figure it out on her own. Was she just playing into the rookie's ego?

"This model should unscrew." The officer pointed to several spots on the shaft. "The first thing I want to check is that the rubber tip is pushed on the whole way. They come loose from wear and tear."

Jake eased forward to get a better look at the proceedings. He wondered if it would be possible to hollow out a hiding spot in the cane's shaft. He was old enough to make it an acceptable part of a disguise or a permanent part of his persona.

Bellevue tugged, and the rubber tip came off with a slight "pop." She ran a finger around its inside and rolled it between the palms of her hands. "Still flexible," she announced. "That's good. They can get brittle."

It was only a cane, Jake thought, but everyone had stopped to watch the young officer at work, as if it was the most important item in the world. She laid the tip on the back of the easy chair, then grasped the metal joint in the middle of the shaft and twisted. Nothing happened.

"Huh. I wonder if someone stripped the threads." She tightened her grasp and tried again. The joints didn't budge.

After wiping her hands on her pants and adjusting her grip, Bellevue twisted the shaft one more time. The metal parts groaned as they loosened, but didn't break free. She grunted as she tried again. This time, the connector turned, and a smile broke out on the young cop's face. "Finally!"

"A muscle man must have assembled that," Harmony said.

Or someone trying to hide something. Jake kept the thought to himself. No one in the room was safe from suspicion.

"I'm afraid to take the top off." Bellevue ran her hand over the decorative handle that resembled a rose. "I don't want to break it."

Harmony shook her head. "Not a problem. I've always thought it seemed loose, like it was the wrong size. But it's pretty, so I kept it. I wish I could remember who gave it to me."

It wasn't like her to forget that detail. Jake wondered how many other memories she'd misplaced.

"Do you want me to take it off?" Harmony asked.

The young officer hesitated. "I hate to leave a job unfinished. With your permission, I'll do it."

Harmony nodded.

Bellevue rolled her shoulders and bounced the top half of the cane, as if gathering her courage. Then she gently grasped the rose and rotated it.

It turned easily. Too easily, in Jake's opinion, but that was better than not coming off at all. It might have been a trick of the light, but as the rose separated from the shaft, Jake thought he saw a piece of metal fall.

"I'm so sorry," Bellevue said, examining the top. "But it looks fine. See?"

She offered the decorative part to Harmony. While Harmony examined it, Jake lowered himself to the floor, careful not to groan as sore muscles complained. He patted the floor, expecting to find more than dust and the occasional pebble.

Houck joined him. "I saw it, too."

"What?" Thomason asked.

Jake shook his head. "A trick of the light maybe, but it looked like a piece of metal fell."

Houck sat back and surveyed the floor. "Officer, can you lift one foot at a time and let me look underneath them?"

When she followed his instruction, Houck ran his hand across the area, but came up empty. Twice.

Jake wondered if Harmony could handle the task. To delay the inevitable embarrassment, he needed a distraction, and the flashlight on his phone was the perfect foil. "A little extra light might help."

"Do… you need me to move?" Harmony shuffled her right foot.

Jake caught the note of hesitation. In another lifetime, he would have gracefully risen and swooped her off her feet. Not this day. Not with a broken arm.

"Hold on. Let me check around your feet first." He made a show of running his hands across the floor and over her shoes. He didn't expect to find anything because, in a move that would have done Jake proud, Houck had slipped something into the cuff of his dress pants. Jake's best guess was that it was an outdated but still functional government-issued homing device, placed in the cane by Houck. That explained how the agent had been so quick locating Harmony in the hotel room the night of the attack.

He'd been underestimating Houck. No more. But the incident gave Jake the ammo he needed for blackmail.

"Take half a step, Angel," he said, tapping her right knee. He'd play along with the farce—for now.

Her left foot moved forward. From his spot on the floor, Jake noticed how unnatural the step was. Too stiff, and her foot barely came off the floor. How would she handle the other foot?

Harmony had it figured out. She put her hand on Bellevue's shoulder and pushed. The bulk of her negligible weight ended up there instead of on her injured leg and foot and enabled her to take a step.

Jake faked taking extra care as he checked the area. He'd used the moment when all eyes had been on Harmony to reach into his pants pocket, where a few coins rattled around.

"Any luck?" Houck asked.

Jake shook his head. "Nothing. Except for this dime." He held it up so the others could see. "It's not old, so I don't imagine it came from the cane. It's not like you can use it to make a phone call or anything. Although people still carry a lucky penny, I've never heard of a lucky dime. I'm guessing one of the crew who worked on the house dropped it." He was counting on that dime to buy him at least one favor from Houck.

"I'm giving up and blaming my imagination." Houck sent him a sharp glance before groaning and pushing himself up off the floor.

Getting down had been one thing, but Jake was stuck with nothing to grab onto to pull himself up.

Thomason must have realized Jake's predicament and offered his hand. "It's hell growing old."

Jake accepted the help, the excuse, and the way to retain his dignity. "I get reminded of that on a regular basis."

Thomason stared into Jake's eyes a few seconds longer than was polite. If he was waiting for Jake to convey a hidden message, he'd be disappointed. Jake had nothing he was willing to share.

Bellevue was reassembling the cane after using a paper towel to wipe the metal parts. "I won't over-tighten it. That way, when you get home, you can take it apart. Just double-check when you're done that the joints are secure."

As the officer handed the cane back to Harmony, Jake considered its uses as a weapon. Could she balance well enough on her good leg to use it like a baseball bat? Once upon a time, he'd let her believe that she'd taken him down using a self-defense trick she'd learned. It hadn't worked, but he'd played along to make her feel better. He didn't have the luxury of pretending now.

Chapter 13

Cloaked by the musty curtains of his third hotel room, Jake studied the traffic on the street below. He knew every unmarked car owned by the Oak Grove police, and two of them patrolled the neighborhood. Despite their presence, he'd been unable to determine their encrypted channel on the hacker's scanner.

He turned away from the window, walked to the bedside table, and poured a second drink from the bottle Danny had left at the front desk. Doc Gabe would be upset with him, but Jake figured he deserved the break from abstinence. The doc had sighed while he studied the damage to Jake's cast, and muttered something about sending him to a nursing home in Pittsburgh. It had been an empty threat.

Even flirting with Trina and Belinda at the clinic hadn't eased his restlessness, and Jake paced as he sipped his whiskey. He planned meticulously for his heists, analyzing every contingency, leaving room for changing circumstances. It offered him a sense of control. He craved control. The current situation offered none.

He drained the glass and tilted his head up, letting the harsh liquid burn the back of his throat. A small, black spider wove a web where the wall and ceiling met. Jake had heard rumors about the Feds developing the technology to use robotic insects to bug a room, but not that they could spin silk. It seemed safe to ignore the spider.

He resisted the urge to pour another shot and sat on the bed next to the police scanner. Back when he was learning to pick locks, he'd spend hours on the same padlock, figuring out how the pins inside worked, listening to the clicks as they dropped into place, and sensing the slight vibration through his fingertips as they nestled into their spots.

That ability had marked him as one of the best in his prime. He didn't have the touch for the electronic locks that were standard these days, much like the scanner. He sighed and tapped in the number for the next channel. How long would it take him to test all five thousand of them one at a time?

Too long without proper preparation, including food.

By ten that night, Jake hadn't even gotten through the first hundred. Each time he tried a new channel, he had to wait a few minutes to give the scanner time to pick up a conversation. Or not. The method tested every bit of his patience. At this pace, he'd never home in on the right spot.

Despite his frustration, he discovered a certain satisfaction in the process. It was the thrill of the chase. He was getting old, but he still could make his mark. Was this how Harmony and Eli had felt each time they broke a code?

Jake eyed the whiskey on the bedside table. It was tempting, but he wanted to put in a few more hours of testing. He'd save it until he was ready to hit the sack. He stood, stretched, and picked up the empty coffeepot. Third-rate hotel room coffee, made extra dark, would keep him awake.

The glare of spotlights cracked through the acrid haze to illuminate what remained of the front of The Purple Onion. Blue and red strobes from emergency vehicles cast eerie patterns on the surrounding buildings. At the end of the block, cordoned off by police tape, a small crowd surveyed the action, analyzing each move of the firefighters and speculating on motives while avoiding the over-spray from fire hoses.

Jake stood planted in a puddle in the middle of the street, as close as the fire marshal allowed him to get, and wished for that tumbler of whiskey to erase the taste of smoke in his throat and ward off the early morning chill. Now that the fire was out, he had nothing to keep him warm except for the anger burning in his heart.

"Do you suppose they'll let me keep the bar's sign?" he asked Thomason, who had again played chauffeur and transported Jake to the scene. "I could hang it over the mirror or on the back wall."

"It's a good thing you installed the fire suppression system a few years ago." Thomason stuck his hands in his jacket's pockets. "The entire place would be gone if you hadn't."

"City Hall forced me to jump through fabricated hoops to let it happen. They didn't want me making any improvements. I suspect someone hoped they could find enough issues to condemn the building and close the bar." Jake huffed. "I can imagine the trouble they will give me when I apply for the permits to make repairs. Hell, it would be easier to take the insurance settlement and raze the lot."

"Someone finally figured out a way to run you out of town."

"I said it would be easier to take the payout. That doesn't mean I'll do it. The bar is practically a historical monument, and I'd feel guilty closing it."

"True. It sure makes it look as if you are the target of everything that's been happening, not Harmony. The fire gives Houck the ammo he needs to coerce her into returning to Florida."

"And away from me. What if he's the one who set this up? He's got the right connections. It all started with his arrival."

Thomason straightened. "That's a bold assumption."

"What do we know about him, other than he's got credentials from a tiny government agency no one is familiar with? I don't have the contacts to check him out. All we have is his word."

"Give me a motive."

Jake adjusted his sling. "Money. Reputation. Using this assignment as a steppingstone to a bigger team? Or, and this sounds crazy, he's deep undercover for some foreign organization. Maybe he's the one withholding the files, so Harmony can't figure it out."

"There's a major flaw in that theory—he's had months in Florida to hurt her if he wanted to."

"If you hadn't noticed, she's changed since she got here. She's more alive, more aware, like she's waking up from a long sleep."

"And that makes her a threat." Thomason rubbed the back of his neck. "It's convoluted enough to make it possible because it's Harmony we're dealing with."

Jake jerked his head towards a fireman he'd noticed lingering nearby, rolling up a hose. "And one we shouldn't be discussing in public."

"You'll get me the security footage as soon as you can, right?" Thomason asked.

Jake admired his quick change of topic. "I should be able to retrieve the file. I'll send you a link to the cloud storage site."

"When the other businesses on the block open, we'll have officers reach out to them. Unless a ghost is responsible, there's bound to be something useful."

"Or a spook."

"Hold that thought," Thomason warned in a low voice as an officer raised the police tape and allowed a car through. "Here comes the chief."

❄ ❄ ❄

"Am I a suspect?" Jake asked, looking up from the screen of his watch.

Thomason set a foam cup of coffee on the desk in front of Jake. He'd commandeered this empty office at the station so Jake would have a quiet place to review the bar's security footage. "Not at the moment. Your alibi is solid, and it wouldn't make any sense for you to start a fire without turning off the suppression system."

The wooden chair screeched against the bare tile floor as Jake pushed it away from the desk. He picked up the coffee and took a deep swallow. "I had to go through hell and high water to have the system installed."

"Did a local company do the work?"

"No, one out of Cleveland. They also set up the system for the bar up there. The owner owed me a favor."

Jake rolled his shoulders to ease the ache in his back. He'd fallen asleep on the floor next to the hacking device.

"His son threw a party and ran out on the tab," he continued, "but dropped his phone on the way out. I called 'Dad' in the contacts and let him know what happened. Next day, Dad came to settle the bill, we got talking, and he ended up selling me the system at a reduced price."

"How about the security system?"

"A company out of Pittsburgh. Same one I use for the systems in the homes I remodel. They give me a discount for being a repeat customer."

"I'd like to speak to someone there. See if they can come up with any additional info. You haven't spotted anything, right? None of the officers who reviewed the footage caught anything of interest."

Jake grimaced. "Not a darn thing. I keep telling myself when I view the firebombing on a bigger screen I'll catch the culprit, but if your guys didn't see something out of the ordinary, my chances are next to impossible."

"Which points to someone who knows the system. A disgruntled ex-employee? Or a current employee who has been stealing from you and hoped to cover their tracks?"

"None of my guys would do that." Jake stood and started pacing. "Unless I can get in and run an inventory, I can't prove it."

"Be patient. The fire department is bringing in an expert and they won't release the scene until he finishes collecting the samples he needs. Chief Santos has posted officers both front and back, so the building is secure." Thomason dropped his voice. "Is there anything in there you are worried about?"

Jake had sold off the few items in his "treasure chest" in the basement—including a GPS tracker that tapped into the traffic signal network—a few weeks earlier. He forced a thoughtful frown. "Only a hundred-year-old bottle of scotch I'm saving for a special occasion. That and I don't know how much cash business Danny did last night. We didn't discuss it when I called him this morning, but it should be in the safe."

Thomason raised an eyebrow. "Is the scotch in the safe or your desk?"

"No offense, Detective, but I'd prefer to not reveal its location unless it's necessary for the investigation." Jake grinned.

"Agreed. We wouldn't want anyone to be tempted to hunt for it."

Jake paused in the middle of raising the coffee cup to

his lips. "Putting aside my previous theory, what if the fire was set as a diversion by someone wanting to rob the bar? Someone who didn't realize I had a security system?"

"Good thought. It's easier to believe than the idea that Houck is orchestrating everything. I'll request the officers and fire official check for any signs of attempted forced entry."

"As much as I'd like to blame Houck, I wonder who he is working with. He hasn't been in town long enough to have the insider's knowledge he'd need. Like knowing just where to dump a stolen car."

"I don't like where you are going." Thomason leaned forward and crossed his arms on the scarred metal desk. "Do you want to close the door before you finish your thought?"

Jake reached backwards and pushed the office door. It closed with a satisfying "clunk." "He's got at least one tracker on Harmony. At least, he did, until it fell out of her cane."

"What?"

"I can't prove it." Jake shrugged. "He got his hands on it first, but that explains how he found Harmony at the hotel the night she slipped away from her guards."

"And?" Thomason prompted.

"That doesn't explain how you were tracked the night we were followed. That wasn't accidental."

"One incidence is pretty flimsy to base a theory on. That could have been a coincidence."

Jake grinned. "What would Harmony say? She doesn't believe in coincidences. And it wasn't once—it clicked when we were rewinding the video to listen for the shots. You rewound it too far back, and that's when I saw it."

"Saw what? Spit it out."

"The cop car cruising the street a few minutes before the bad guys showed up the first time. That doesn't feel like coincidence."

Chapter 14

"Harmony is untouchable," Jake pointed out, "Despite the gaps in her security. What does that tell you?"

"What gaps?" Thomason asked.

They had left the police station with the excuse of getting lunch. Now, they were sitting in a pavilion at the park, eating takeout from the Dairy Barn. With the cooler weather and school in session, they could talk with no one overhearing, and no need to worry about listening devices.

"I'm not a security expert," Thomason continued, "but what is Houck missing?"

Jake pulled a pickle off his burger. "Think about what one person could accomplish with a sniper rifle. Are you aware Harmony is a James Bond fan? Or used to be, anyway. She got me to read the books back before Eli was in her life. When I was in prison, I read lots of books like them. Trust me, a determined attacker could hurt her. Which tells me if someone is after her, they want her alive."

"So, the attacks have been to scare you away?"

"At least distract me, so I'm not guarding Harmony."

"And you suspect someone in the police department is responsible? Aren't you biased?" Thomason shoved his leftovers into the bag.

"Absolutely. Yet here I am, sharing my suspicions with you."

"You've given me an impossible choice. Investigate my coworkers on the sly and without my chief's permission, or decide you're crazy, leaving Harmony open to attack. And you."

"It's not fair of me to drag you into this. It could mean the end of your career and I'm a low-life ex-con and not worth it."

"You could be the key to ensuring that Harmony is safe and can stay here in Oak Grove where she wants to be. Like I said, an impossible choice."

"For me, too." Jake clasped his hands behind his head and studied an old cobweb in the rafters of the pavilion. "Because this could escalate."

❄ ❄ ❄

Jake had made it a rule to never own a gun after his first few encounters with cops. Even when the laws changed to allow certain ex-cons to have their rights restored, he hadn't applied. It wasn't worth the effort. Besides, no authority would give a convicted cop-beater the right to bear arms. With the bar closed, his primary weapon—information—had vanished.

He and Danny stood across the street from The Purple

Onion, observing the fire inspector collect samples of the debris while a stream of cars rolled by. The gossips were having a field day. Jake watched for any vehicle that seemed suspicious—the perpetrator returning to the scene. So far, he hadn't spotted anything.

"I'm surprised the investigators are putting this much effort into it," Danny said. "I figured they'd slap a condemned sign on what's left of the front door and call it good."

"I'm glad they're taking it seriously. The insurance company has already called me about getting a police report."

"How long will we be closed?"

"A couple of months, once I get the permits."

"Well, shit," Danny groaned. "Guess I better start looking for a new job. Unemployment won't cover my bills."

"How do you feel about working in Cleveland? I've been ignoring the business up there, and the guys are putting in extra hours to cover my absence. You can stay in my rooms above the bar."

The move would cut Jake off from another contact with the Oak Grove gossip network, but it was the right thing to do. It would also get Danny out of town so he wouldn't get hurt in a future attack on Jake. "I've put out feelers with other bars in town to see if we can get spots for everyone else. I don't want anyone to take a financial hit from this."

"Besides you."

Jake huffed. "It's gonna hurt, no lie. You might have to wear pink tassels and help me draw in a younger crowd."

"At least make them blue, not pink. And you can hire my Aunt Tootsie as a waitress. Put her into a skimpy outfit and let her serve drinks."

"She's pushing what, 90?" Jake chuckled. "The college kids wouldn't know how to react if she started yelling at them to watch their language and settle down."

Danny laughed. "I bet her tips would be great. They'd be afraid to not leave her cash."

A rusty pickup pulled onto the street, fitting in perfectly with the surroundings, and Jake dismissed it as not holding a threat. Then, right in front of them, the brakes screeched, and the passenger side door was flung open.

"Get in," a woman yelled.

"Angel?" Jake hesitated, then nodded towards Danny, and climbed into the truck.

She didn't wait for him to close the door before taking off. "Hold on. I don't know how much time we have until Doan realizes I'm gone. He thinks I'm taking a nap."

The tires squealed as they went around the corner. Jake struggled to fasten his seat belt.

"Where are we going? And how did you get away from Houck?"

Harmony brushed a cobweb out of her hair, wiping her hand on the seat. "Last time I checked, cell coverage on the Outlook was terrible. I figure that will delay Doan."

"Ha! You *are* aware he is tracking you."

"I suspected it. When did you find out?"

Jake grasped the dashboard as she made a sharp right. "Yesterday. When Officer Bellevue took apart your cane.

I planned to use the info as a bargaining chip."

"Sorry to ruin your plans." She glanced his way. "Since this truck belongs to Marion Nowak next door, and she hasn't driven it for a month, and I wasn't sure it would start, I'm willing to bet it's not tagged. We hatched this plan this morning when I was out pretending to work in the rose garden, and she came over to gossip and told me about the fire."

"I'm more worried about your shoes or purse. If you were going into hiding, those are the first things I'd make you get rid of."

Harmony pushed her small handbag towards him. "Once upon a time, I found a tracker that was disguised as breath mints. The technology has gotten better, but have at it."

"You still haven't told me how you got away," Jake said as he inspected the clasp and seams.

"Out the basement. The alarm is broken." She sped up as they passed the faded city limit sign. "But if you've been keeping track of Eli and me all these years, I bet you knew that."

"Who do you think has been putting fresh batteries in the fake? By the way, where is your phone? I want to take out the sim card."

She chuckled. "On my bed. I overheard Doan telling Freddie that he has an alert that goes off if it goes dark."

"I need to get you a burner. I don't like the idea of you being out of contact."

"Thanks. It feels weird being without it."

They reached the turnoff for the Outlook, which was nothing more than a parking area at the top of a hill outside of town, but a barricade—a sawhorse with a solitary blinking yellow light—blocked the middle of the road. "I heard something about a washout a few weeks ago, when we had that three-day storm," Jake said.

She revved the engine. "It would be a shame to back out now."

"Stick to what's left of the pavement as long as you can. That way, they can't trace your tire tracks."

Harmony steered a path around the barrier. "How's the hunt going?"

"Nothing yet." Jake switched his gaze from the increasingly rough road back to her purse. "So, why are you dragging me out here? I would have come to you."

A wicked grin played on her face. "This is more fun. Besides, I didn't want Doan to know. He's been on me all morning about returning to Florida. The fire has him worked up."

"Rightfully so. He's supposed to protect you."

"From what? You're the one being targeted."

"I've come to the same conclusion."

"And that's why I wanted to talk to you."

They had reached their destination. The unpaved parking lot was mostly a mud puddle, and Harmony chose the one dry spot that offered a view of the valley below, as well as the road. On a sunny day, with the trees in full color, the scenery looked like something out of a painting, but they weren't here to sightsee.

"You find a bug yet?" she asked as she turned off the truck.

"No. If there is one, it's smaller than anything I've dealt with."

"Let me look. I haven't bothered with it when I was behaving."

"Or Houck figured your cell phone would be enough of a tracker. Bad thing to assume."

"He's fairly good at his job, from what I can tell." She flipped through a small pack of tissues and set it aside. "Except for getting me the files I've requested."

Jake held up a tube of lipstick and took off the cap to reveal a deep scarlet interior. "This doesn't seem like your color."

She snatched it out of his hand. "Eli bought it for me as a joke. I haven't been able to get rid of it. "

There had been a time when she didn't wear makeup. "Check it out, anyway," Jake said. "To be on the safe side."

"Paranoid, much? I guess you have a right to be." Still, she took the lid off and peered inside, rolled the lipstick up and down, and ran her fingers over the case. "See? Nothing."

He handed her a pill container. "I don't know what you're taking, what's real and what might be a fake."

She shrugged. "It's vitamins, mostly. I'm weaning myself off the pain pills. I don't like the way they slow down my reflexes."

"Have you tried a different kind?" Jake had a limited knowledge of drugs. He'd refused to deal in them his entire career, even given the profit-making opportunities. That hadn't stopped him from using them occasionally.

"This is my fourth prescription. They all do the same thing. On my worst days, I can't think straight. I'd rather live with the pain." She hesitated. "Don't tell anyone. My doctors are overly protective."

"Maybe it's time for you to see a new doctor."

"That's part of what this move is about. How do I fire my current ones when they literally saved my life?"

Jake picked up her now-empty purse and turned it upside down. "We appear to be in the clear. Now for your shoes."

"First, tell me who your enemy is and how I can help you."

"I don't want to involve you, Angel, any more than you are."

"Tell me."

Jake sighed. She'd worm it out of him one way or another. "The rumor mill claims that some of the police force are doing what they can to run the less-desirable citizens of Oak Grove out of town. Thomason isn't involved. When Houck arrived, he made a point of telling me to stay away from you."

"And you think he's teamed up with these bad cops to get you to leave?"

"That's pure speculation."

"Has anyone taken their concerns to Chief Santos?"

"New chief, new cops. There's no trust. And no one wants to be on the wrong side of a government agency."

"They don't know me very well, do they?" Harmony grinned.

"You shouldn't get involved, Angel. It's too risky."

She stared out the side window. "What do I have left to lose?"

She'd never been homeless. Or worried about where her next meal would come from. Jake stayed quiet, leaving her to her thoughts.

"So, what's your plan?" she asked suddenly.

"I don't have one. I only put the pieces together today. What I haven't figured out is how the threat to you fits in, except for bringing Houck to town."

"Maybe I'm not in any danger and that's why Houck can't produce the files."

Jake patted her knee and left his hand sitting there, as if the movement had strained his damaged arm. "That's wishful thinking. If there isn't a threat, why would Houck be assigned to you?"

"I've been trying to figure that out. I've only got one theory—'they' and she used her fingers to make air quotes, "want me to keep working for them, and this is their way to control my choices."

There was no safe way to ask the question. "How would that work without Eli?"

She clutched the steering wheel with both hands until her knuckles turned white. "Pair me with someone else."

"And there's the missing piece."

"You say that so calmly."

"Look at the big picture, Angel." He twisted so he could use his right hand to touch her cheek. "As long as I'm around, your security clearance is threatened. They have to get rid of me."

Chapter 15

The first drops of a predicted afternoon shower struck the windshield of the old truck as it rumbled down the road. It wasn't much more than a dirt path in a few spots, and Jake hoped the heaviest rainfall would hold off until he and Harmony got back to paved road.

Danny had called, telling Jake the fire inspector wanted to talk with him in person. He wasn't in a hurry. He and Harmony had more to talk about.

"Can't you just say no?" he asked.

Harmony's lips drew into a taut line. "Yes. Will they accept it as an answer? Doubtful. That's not how they operate."

"That changes everything."

"What do you have in mind?"

Jake's grin stretched from ear to ear. "How do you feel about having a new roommate?"

"Doan will hate it," Harmony said as she steered around a downed tree limb. With the addition of gusty wind and rain, the downhill drive was becoming hazardous.

Jake chuckled. "That's the point. He'll need to play nice, and if we are together all the time, he won't have as much opportunity to plot behind your back."

"Or yours."

"Especially mine. That will drive him up a wall."

"It will also give him the ability to monitor your comings and goings, possibly setting you up for another 'accident'."

"I'm more worried about him tracking my internet communications, since we'll be sharing your connection." Jake absentmindedly rotated the watch on his wrist. "I can adjust my security level, but I don't know how much training agents receive in technology."

Harmony glanced at him. "No worries. The best guy in the business owes me a huge favor. The least Lando can do is set things up so Doan isn't able to track you electronically. He'll never make up for allowing Doan to hide undercover at the office."

"And you remind him of that every chance you get."

"It's time he remembers who is in charge."

"Welcome back, Angel."

She slammed on the brakes and threw the truck into park. Jake used his good arm to stop himself from hitting the dash.

"Everyone has been protecting me. Coddling me. Wrapping me in bubble wrap. Who knew that putting me in danger was the way to bring me back to life?"

"It doesn't surprise me. I've always said you had a

natural flair for excitement, no matter how you tried to deny it."

"A few weeks ago, I would have said you were crazy."

"A few weeks ago, I would have agreed. Thing is, Eli was perfect for you, and you were perfect for him. He offered you a mix of danger and safety. You kept him on his toes and didn't let him hide behind his computer code and ignore real life." He wiped away the tears trickling down her cheeks. "That doesn't mean you aren't welcome in my bed anytime."

A smile lit her face. "And there's the Jake who had disappeared."

"He was hiding in sheep's clothing to throw Houck off track. Too bad it didn't work."

"Are you going to let him loose when you move in?"

"Do you want me to?"

"I'm not ready for full-force Jake yet."

Jake chuckled. "I'll take it easy on you, then."

She shifted the truck back into drive and resumed the downhill trip. The rain eased up, but she took her time negotiating around puddles and potholes.

"Do you suppose Doan has called in the National Guard, yet?" she asked as they reached the main road at the bottom.

"Does he normally check up on you while you're sleeping?"

"Tossing and turning, you mean? Not that I've caught him."

"Then maybe he isn't aware that you're missing."

"I'll give him credit. He seems to have a sixth sense about it."

"Or it was the tracker."

"We'll see. Heads up, we have a cop car behind us."

"You know the drill. They've got no reason to stop us. Just stick to the speed limit, use your turn signals, and maintain your lane."

"Yep, I've got it in control. You taught me well, Jake."

They made it back to the bar without being stopped, although the cruiser stayed with them the entire way. When Harmony pulled into a spot down the street from the bar, it stayed on course and disappeared around the next corner.

"I'm assuming Houck has been notified of our presence," Jake said as he unfastened his seatbelt. "Last chance to change your mind."

"Give up and go back to Florida? Not happening. Oak Grove is my home, and this is my first step to reclaiming it."

"Then let the fun begin." Jake hopped out of the truck, waved to Danny, and strolled around to the driver's side to open Harmony's door. "Do you need a hand getting out?"

She eyed the distance to the ground. "I'm not used to vehicles this high."

He got as close to her as he could. "Put your arm on my shoulder and use me as support. I'd lift you out, but…" It was better this way. If he got his arms around her, he wouldn't want to let go. She wasn't ready for that. Hell, he wasn't ready.

She swung both legs through the opening, but her feet dangled several inches above the street. She grasped the door frame with one hand and Jake's arm with the other, and lowered herself to the ground, her right foot hitting the pavement first. Before letting go, she paused, settling her stance.

"My cane is behind the seat. Would you mind getting it for me?"

Her voice seemed strained. "Are you all right?" Jake asked.

"I'm fine."

"You're lying." He reached past her and found her cane, examining it before he handed it to her.

"Drop it, Jake." she said sharply.

"Yes, ma'am." He raised his hands in surrender.

Danny met them halfway down the block. "Good news, Boss. We're cleared to board up the place and start cleanup."

"I'll get someone to bring over plywood if you want to schedule the crew for cleanup work. I'll pay their standard rate plus a bonus. That'll help make up for the tips they're losing." Another hit to his wallet, but it was only fair.

"The inspector also said we need to dump the booze, even the unopened bottles, because they can be contaminated by the chemicals that were sprayed."

Jake winced. "Ouch. I hope insurance covers inventory."

"Glad that's your problem, not mine." He stuck his hand out towards Harmony. "I'm Danny. Jake inherited me when he bought the bar. You must be Angel."

She grinned and shook his hand. "Call me Harmony. Only Jake gets to call me Angel, and some days even he doesn't get away with it."

"If she's angry, she'll insist on Mrs. Duprie. And if she's really upset, it's Mrs. Duprie-Hennessey," Jake explained.

"And what does the federal agent coming our way call you?" Danny asked.

Her back straightened, and her chin lifted. She was preparing to do battle.

"Take a deep breath, Angel," Jake urged.

"I've got this. Watch me."

Jake stifled a grin. Houck didn't know what he was in for.

"Hennessey." Houck growled. "I should arrest you for interfering with a federal operation."

Harmony rolled her eyes before turning to face Houck. "I'm not aware I'm breaking any laws, Agent. Care to enlighten me?"

His jaw dropped. "Not you, Mrs. Duprie. Him." He waved a hand towards Jake.

"May I remind you, to you it's Mrs. Duprie-Hennessey. Perhaps you should remember where my loyalties lie. Just a clue—not with you. I promised to cooperate with FASS as long as the agency supplied me with the information I requested, and they haven't. Therefore, our agreement is null and void. I expect you to move out of my home as quickly as possible. Tonight is good, but tomorrow is acceptable. You have overstayed your welcome."

Holy shit. Jake had never seen her like this. He was glad he wasn't in Houck's shoes.

"I won't allow you to put yourself in danger," Houck said after a long pause.

"Are you going to stick with that story? Because you haven't given me any proof, and the only person who needs protection is Jake. Who I've convinced to move in."

The agent's face turned deep red, and his eyes narrowed to a slit. "I won't allow it."

Harmony raised her cane and poked it at him. He backed up. "You have no authority over me, Agent. Unless my status has changed in the past two years, I may outrank you. I'm done playing by your rules, now I'm creating my own. You can either follow my lead or I will have you removed from the case."

Could she do that? As much as he was enjoying it, Jake decided the argument had gone on long enough and put his hand on Harmony's arm. "You're attracting attention. You need to take this discussion somewhere private."

She nodded. "You're right. Agent, we can meet back at the house to discuss future arrangements. Jake, are you coming?"

Jake weighed his options. For his own amusement, he wanted to watch Harmony deal with Houck, but he had to start cleaning the bar and collecting personal items. "I need to take care of business first. Do you have supper plans? I'll pick up something from Mama D's."

"Thank you, that would be nice."

"I'll give you a ride back, so you don't have to wait for him," Houck said.

Harmony's eyebrows arched. "Wrong again, Agent. I have a vehicle. You can follow me to the house." She pointed towards the truck.

Jake predicted another argument starting. "Drive careful, Angel." He hoped she'd get the hint.

She grinned. "Don't forget the extra breadsticks."

❈ ❈ ❈

Jake had designed this third-floor room when the house was being remodeled a quarter of a century ago. He'd combined two small bedrooms and added a picture window overlooking the city and, in good weather, framing spectacular sunsets. Tonight, wind drove rain against the glass.

In the dark, he stared at the string of lights that lined the street and listened to the sounds coming from the next room where Houck was packing up his equipment. Jake had brought nothing but one change of clothing and a few toiletries. And, of course, a bottle of whiskey. He had no intention of making this stay last more than a day or two, unless he talked Harmony into making it forever. He had no hope for that.

She was tucked into her room on the first floor, where Jake couldn't get to her in a hurry in case of an emergency. He'd fix that soon enough, and spend the night in one of the comfortable chairs in the living room. There had been many times when he'd slept in worse places.

The knock on the door was expected. Houck had equipment in this room, too. Jake emptied the glass down his throat before answering.

"Agent," he said, nodding.

"Hennessey."

Jake stepped aside. "I'll stay out of your way. Are you moving across the street?"

"You put her up to this." Houck's eyes narrowed.

"I presume you didn't know her before the accident."

"What does that have to do with it?"

"You never saw how her mind works. She's a natural at seeing patterns where the rest of us miss them. When she gets fixated on an idea, it's hard to get her to focus on anything else. You broke one of her cardinal rules. You've blocked her from access to information she needs to analyze the problem."

"I don't understand."

Jake strode across the room, poured another glass of whiskey, and stared out the window with his back to the agent. "She and I had a conversation this afternoon. Are you aware she's stopped taking her pain pills? My theory is they interfered with her thought process. She's coming out of the fog she's been in and has less patience for nonsense."

"That doesn't decrease the threat against her," Houck pointed out.

"What threat? I'm the only one being attacked. Funny how those attacks started once you showed up. As Harmony says, she doesn't believe in coincidence."

"Are you accusing me of orchestrating them?"

Chapter 16

"Just stating the facts. Trying to see the patterns that Harmony does." Jake watched the reflection in the window as Houck dismantled his equipment. Although it would bring a nice profit on the black market, none of it was the newest technology, so Jake hadn't touched it.

"For all I know, you're the one setting up these attacks, and using them to manipulate Mrs. Duprie-Hennessey," the agent said.

Jake swiveled to face the agent. "Interesting theory, and easy to disprove. Take yesterday. Are you claiming I anticipated Harmony and the rest of you showing up at the house? And I set up the drive-by shooting? It doesn't fit the pattern."

"Yet you've wormed your way into an invitation to stay here."

"Instead of leaving town in defeat? Someone doesn't know me very well."

"Why do you stay? I've seen your official books. You aren't getting rich, from either the bar or your construction business."

A lifetime ago, he'd come to steal a rare book from Harmony. One it turned out she didn't have after all. In the process, he'd fallen in love with her. Then, he'd stuck around to protect her and fallen in love with the town and its inhabitants. None of which he'd share with Houck.

"Oak Grove has a strange effect on people," he said. "Either you love it and stick around, or you hate it and leave. I'm in the 'love it' category."

Houck slammed shut the metal lid of a storage container. "I don't believe it for a second. You've got an agenda, and I *will* find out what it is."

❄ ❄ ❄

He woke to a heavy cloth being slipped over his body, jerked upright, and grabbed the hand that hovered near his throat. Harmony tumbled across his chest.

"Whoa there, Jake, you fell asleep. What are you doing down here?"

She tried to pull herself away, but Jake pushed aside the blanket and wrapped one arm around her, so her head was resting on his good shoulder. He should have let her go, but it was an opportunity he couldn't pass up.

"The resident ghost was restless, so I came down to read." It was partly true, and a book lay on the nearby table to prove it.

She sat up. "I haven't heard the ghost since I got here. I thought it was gone."

"I wasn't serious."

"I am."

"That's not logical, Angel."

She supported herself with the arm of the chair, twisted her way off his lap, and stood. A momentary grimace was replaced with a forced smile. "Yeah, I know. That doesn't stop me from believing."

This discussion was going nowhere. "What are you doing awake?"

"Typical night. Even the sleep meds don't let me sleep through the night, so I stopped taking them, too."

"Without talking to your doctor?"

She stared at the floor. "Don't give me a hard time, Jake. I'd rather feel the pain than not feel at all."

It had to be said. "Even the pain of losing Eli?" he asked softly.

"Especially the pain of losing Eli," she answered, her voice tense. She walked over to the mantel and turned on the masking device. "Now that I have some of the files I need."

Jake blinked. "Houck got them for you? Why didn't he use them as blackmail to stay?"

"Not Houck." Harmony shook her head. "An old friend who works for Homeland Security in DC got them for me. She's researching Houck and his chain of command. Her experience tells her the whole thing is fishy."

"And he doesn't know this?"

"I have my secrets."

"You never cease to amaze me, Angel. Can I help?" Information was power. What could he learn from those files?

Harmony snorted. "There's no way I'm giving you

access. Not even a peek. Your job is to make sure no one walks in on me when I'm working with them. Not Houck, not Freddie, not you. Agreed?"

The light in her room had stayed on far too late, not that Jake had stayed awake the whole time. He'd dozed, confident in his ability to wake at the slightest noise. So, he was ready to hand her a hot cup of coffee when she limped to the kitchen mid-morning.

He couldn't tell if her swollen eyes were due to lack of sleep or if she'd been crying. He took the coward's way out and ignored them. "Houck is still here," he informed her in an almost-whisper.

She nodded. "I figure he's come up with a last-minute delaying tactic. I'll handle it after I get some coffee in my system. It's easy enough to cut his network access."

Jake grinned. "That's brutal."

"Not as brutal as blocking signals in and out of the house. Including cell phones and your fancy-dancy watch."

"You can do that?"

"It's technically possible." Moisture pooled in her eyes. "Eli used to joke about adapting this house so that when we took a few days off, no one could bother us."

Jake ignored the threatened tears. "Which reminds me, I need to get you a burner."

"I won't need it once Agent Houck is out of the house."

"Think again. Who knows what Houck added to your phone?"

"Nothing. My phone is locked down hard."

Jake didn't trust anything the government touched. He wouldn't argue with her now, but a new phone would be in her future.

They turned at the sound of approaching footsteps. Jake moved in front of Harmony until Houck appeared in the doorway.

"Good morning, Mrs. Duprie-Hennessey," he said, ignoring Jake.

"Good morning. How long until you get moved out?"

"I talked to the special agent in charge. He'll get the agency lawyers to draw up the paperwork to have you put in protective custody. I'm not leaving."

"Is that how you want to play this game? My lawyers will demand any agency files backing up the request become part of the record. Which means I will have access to them. If I feed my media contacts a story about a secretive government group harassing a grieving widow, how will that look? And I can't imagine any judge in the area siding with that agency over a local girl coming home to heal after a tragedy in her life. Think carefully. You may believe you have me cornered in a game of checkers, but I'm playing chess. Checkmate, Agent."

She was good. Real good. Jake stood back and admired her as she talked. She didn't need his help. Houck's face flushed, and Jake wasn't sure if it was from embarrassment, anger, or a combination.

"I only want what's best for you," Houck sputtered.

"Best for me? Or best for whatever agency requested this charade? Are they afraid I might have a memory lapse and slip and share privileged information with someone I shouldn't? Or are they wanting to coerce me to work for them again now that I am recovering?"

What did she find in the files? Or was she making educated guesses based on her experience?

"I take my duties seriously," Houck snapped. "Even if it means protecting you from yourself. Or your supposed friends."

The glance he shot at Jake might have withered a less confident person, but Jake wasn't afraid. "Angel has lots of friends," he said. "Some might not meet your standards, but they'd do everything they can to help her, from the retired cops patrolling the neighborhood to the guys from the wrong side of town she's never met, keeping an eye on the woods behind the house."

"I wasn't aware, Jake. About the folks out back. They're doing that for me?" Harmony asked.

He shrugged. "A few of them owe me a favor. Some are doing it because it makes them feel they are contributing. Others are in it for the potential excitement. There isn't coverage all day every day anymore, but every bit helps."

"Tell them I say thank you. I'd do it myself, but I suppose that isn't a good idea."

"I'll pass the word along. They've also cleaned up the garbage back there. Thought you'd appreciate that."

"I always wanted to do something with that lot. After this is over, I'll have to look into it." She took a sip of her coffee and turned to glare at Houck. "When will this be over, Agent?"

"You know how this works. It's over when it's over."

"Except when it's never over. I refuse to live that way. So, go guard me from a distance and stay out of my life until you have hard evidence of a threat you can share."

Houck turned to Jake. "Talk some sense into her. Or did you plant this idea in her head?"

"Angel has never been fond of men interfering in her life, thinking they need to protect her. She even turned down my offer to act as her bodyguard once upon a time. It shocked me when she agreed to you staying here."

Harmony grinned. "I remember that. I figured you were using it as an excuse to get into my bed."

Jake cocked his head. "Well, that too. That was before you and Eli figured out you were perfect for each other."

He waited for the tears. They didn't come. She'd shifted back to her business persona.

"I want you out of my house, Agent. As far as I can tell, you being here hasn't aided the investigation. You'll be just as productive sitting on the front steps of the house across the street. If you don't leave, I will file an official complaint against you for trespassing."

❄ ❄ ❄

Jake was restless. Bored. Frustrated. Everything that could be done to secure The Purple Onion was done, and now he was waiting for the insurance company to process his claim before filing for the permits to start repairs. The insurance company was waiting for the police report. To add to his issues, Houck's presence across the street was a mosquito bite he couldn't scratch.

It had been three days since Harmony had kicked out the agent, and Jake spent much of that time playing butler, cook, dishwasher, and bodyguard while she spent her time behind a closed door. He'd hear her muttering to herself, but she'd turn off her monitor whenever he entered. When she emerged from her room, her eyes were reddened, and she would barely speak to him. Several times, he heard her talking to someone, but he could never catch enough of the conversation to gain any useful information.

He should drop by the Cleveland bar, reassure everyone he was alive and healing, and check how Danny was settling in. His gut wouldn't let him leave Oak Grove.

From the kitchen window, he watched a shadow moving in the woods behind the house. Jake strained to identify its caster, but the person wore dark clothing and slipped from one tree trunk to the next. Likely a veteran that frequented the bar. If Marty's stories were true, he'd trained with a special forces group, but hadn't made the final cut. Corry had been assigned to a hotspot in Africa for a year. The figure in the woods might be either.

"Any chance I can talk you into making me a cup of coffee?" Harmony asked, taking off her glasses and rubbing her eyes as she limped into the kitchen. Jake wasn't sure if her eyes were red from too much time in front of a computer screen or if she'd been crying again.

"You should eat," he said.

"I should, but I don't feel like it."

"You didn't feel like breakfast this morning or supper last night."

"Don't nag me. I grabbed myself a breakfast bar while you went to your doctor's appointment yesterday. How did it go?"

"Best news is, from now on I can do video visits for my checkups. I'm cleared to resume most normal activities, like driving, but I still can't get the cast wet. That gives me an idea—why don't we get out of the house and grab something to eat at a restaurant? Head towards Pittsburgh, leave town for a couple of hours. It would be good for you."

"Houck won't be happy."

"The only thing that will make him happy is for you to return to Florida."

She shook her head. "I can't find anything in the files to justify the move."

"That's because you're looking for evidence." With one finger, Jake tapped her forehead. "You're ignoring emotion. Does Houck have a girlfriend? Is he up for promotion and this assignment puts him out of the running? Does he dread winter? Maybe it's as simple as he's tired of not getting any downtime."

"I hadn't considered that."

"Besides, I need to take the rental car I'm using back and get mine. I want to pick up a new burner phone to replace the one I gave you while we are at it."

"Will that work? Houck will follow us."

Jake grinned. "We've removed the bugs Houck had planted on you and we'll be switching cars three times. Odds are your car and the rental have trackers, but my car won't. Let's see if he can keep up."

Chapter 17

"So far, so good." Jake held the passenger door of the rental open for Harmony. "Now the fun begins."

They'd eaten a late lunch at a diner a mile off the interstate, small enough that Houck wasn't able to hide his presence. Jake had stuck to the speed limit, signaled his turns, and made it easy for Houck to follow. Now he was ready to change the rules.

"It was nice of you to pay Houck's bill, Jake So, what do you have up your sleeve.?" Harmony asked through the open car door as she fastened her seatbelt.

He leaned over and felt around under the rear bumper. When he stood, he held a small black device in his hand. "If I stick it on Houck's car, how long will it take him to figure it out?"

"Too late. That's him coming out now," she said.

"Oh, well." Jake tossed the tracker into the air and caught it on its downward fall. "It would be a shame if it fell off on its own. If I hit a pothole or two, it could happen."

"Living dangerously?"

Always. "I'll take reasonable precautions. You still carry a gun?"

"My hands weren't steady enough, so I gave it up."

"Smart. I'll add it to my calculations."

"What calculations?"

"It won't make a difference if nothing happens. And I don't expect anything will." He slid into the driver's seat.

Harmony closed her door and tugged on her seatbelt to adjust it. "You're planning for it, anyway."

Always. He hit the button, and the green light that showed the car was running came on. "We'll take the scenic route."

The old oak trees along this street had shed most of their leaves and the pavement was covered in a brown, sodden litter that hid the cracks and bumps. Near the end of the street were several Victorian homes Jake figured Harmony would appreciate.

"I considered buying one of these as a project a few years back," he said as he slowed to remove his sling and so Harmony could gawk. "Then a big-name flipping company came in and snatched it up. They look great, but I know the quality of their work. A lot of little things need to be redone."

"That's a shame."

They went over a bump and Jake rolled down his window and pointed towards the house, palming the tracker. A few seconds later, the tracker was no longer in his hand. "No big loss. It was too far from Oak Grove for me to tackle. I can only stretch so far."

"Do you ever take time off?"

He did, but not for reasons he could share. His last vacation had been a cover for stealing an emerald ring. It wasn't of any great value, but it was a way to keep his hand in the game. "I make a point of getting out of town once a year when business is slow."

"You used to send me postcards from your travels."

And they'd been used in an investigation trying to prove he was a drug smuggler. "You're the one who used to go places. How many countries did you explore with Eli?"

She knotted her hands. "Only a few. He preferred to stay in the States to make it easy to get back if there was an emergency at the office."

Jake turned onto a side street without signaling, but going slowly enough for the agent to follow.

"What are you doing?" Harmony asked.

"Two blocks up there's an intersection where we need to stop. The cross street is busy. If things work out, Houck will get stuck."

"That easy?"

It was never that easy. The trick was to have scoped it out ahead of time to make it look easy. "With any luck."

By the time they reached the intersection, Houck had allowed one car to get in between them. A good maneuver for hidden surveillance. Jake flipped on his turn signal and waited for a clear spot in the traffic. When his chance came, he made a clean turn and matched the speed of the rest of the traffic.

"What should I do next, Angel?" He'd taught her a few tricks years ago. Did she remember them?

Her eyes twinkled. "Head down an alley. Or cut through a parking lot to get to the next block. If you want to upset Houck, you can come out at a light and go back the way we came."

"I taught you well," he said solemnly. "Disappearing is enough for the day. We can blame it on traffic, and he can't prove otherwise."

"Where to now?"

"The dealership. I want my car back."

They made the swap, but Jake pulled into an empty parking lot a few blocks away.

"Is there a problem?" Harmony asked.

"If you think I trust Manny the Car King further than I can spit, you're wrong. He sold the same car to two different buyers on the same day, according to my sources. I want to see if he allowed anyone to add a tag to this one."

"Can I help?"

"You take the trunk while I check the undercarriage. We're trying to find things that look out of place."

Five minutes later, Jake picked himself up from where he was lying on the pavement, using the flashlight on his phone to peer under the car. "I haven't found anything. Even the app is coming up blank. How about you, Angel?"

"Nothing." She pulled her head out of the back seat. "Is that good?"

"Houck hasn't shown up yet, and that's our best sign. So, on to buy a burner. There's a strip mall nearby that has helped me before."

"You wave a little cash at them?"

"A lot, actually. With the regulations, it's tougher these days to cover your tracks."

"Why, Jake?"

He blinked. "Why what?"

"Why do you take these precautions? You're a legit businessman, right?"

Most of the time. He shrugged. "Force of habit, I guess. And a dislike of nosy government intruding into my life."

"I've forgotten what that's like." Harmony looked out the side window. "Not having someone peering over my shoulder constantly. Doctors, nurses, agents from one government organization or another. I was hoping to leave that behind."

Jake wanted to reach over and wrap her in a hug. Instead, he started the car. "This is your first step."

He kept one eye on the mirror as he drove the short distance to the strip mall. An unremarkable black car had passed them and set alarm bells off. It was too new, too shiny for this area. Perhaps the driver was taking a shortcut to an unknown destination.

Harmony rubbed the back of her neck and swiveled as far as the seat belt let her. "If I didn't know better, I'd say we're being followed, but no one's behind us."

"Glad your instincts are working. They confirm mine, but I can't locate any threat, either. If we're being shadowed, they're damn good."

"So, what's the plan?"

He didn't have one. "We keep going, with a variation in our route. See if we can pick up what's raising the alarm. Force them to show themselves."

"If anyone can make that work, it's you. How can I help?"

"Watch the side streets and driveways for vehicles that don't fit in. I'll handle the rear."

They didn't talk as Jake executed a series of turns that looped them back towards the car dealership, but his mind was in overdrive. What had he missed? He'd checked Harmony's belongings and found no bugs, her phone was in airplane mode, the car was clean as far as he knew, where else could a tracking device hide?

"Did we imagine it?" she asked, still moving her head from side to side.

"Both of us? It's possible, but I'm going to scratch the burner for this trip. In fact, unless you urgently need to go somewhere else, we should head back to Oak Grove."

"I guess that means no stop at a pawnshop."

"Sorry." Jake checked his mirrors before changing lanes. "Will you call Houck and update him on our location? That should earn us points."

"And provide back-up?"

Or put us back in the path of harm. It'll be an interesting test. "That's the idea. Stay sharp. I'm not convinced we're in the clear."

Harmony gripped the door handle. "Are you trying to scare me?"

"No. That's not my intention. I don't want to mislead you, either."

"I've lost my taste for danger."

"Can't blame you. What you've been through is enough for one lifetime." He checked his mirrors again. There it was, two blocks back. A generic black sedan with tinted windows, but not Houck's. Too far away to raise the alarm. Time to get on a major street and mingle with other drivers.

He drummed his fingers on the steering wheel when they got stuck in a line of traffic behind a school bus. He'd disabled the controls that automatically applied the brakes when the bus sent out a signal, but he wasn't in a hurry and slowed, blending in. Their follower would get stuck, too.

Harmony's phone dinged. "Agent Houck wants another update on our location," Harmony said.

"That's fine. Use your judgment on how often you text him. Did he say where he is?"

The bus turned onto a side street, and Jake picked up speed as Harmony spoke into her phone. He'd lost track of the black sedan, but that meant they'd lost sight of him, too. Once they got to the interstate, a half-mile away, there'd be more room to maneuver if the situation changed.

Harmony's phone dinged again, and she chuckled. "He's looking for the next exit so he can turn around. He assumed we were heading to Pittsburgh."

Jake grinned. "He could have just called and asked."

"And ruin the illusion that he knows what he's doing?"

Harsh, but the truth. "Ask him if he's aware of other agencies operating in our vicinity."

"Do we have a follower?" Harmony flipped down her sun visor and used the mirror to check behind them.

"Check three cars in front of us."

"There are two of them?" she asked, her voice rising a few notes.

"At least. They are popping in and out of my view and I can't watch traffic and keep track of them. It's like playing whack-a-mole."

"I missed them totally."

"You're out of practice, Angel. And a setup like this is rare. It's the first time I've seen it in action."

"Who can put it into play?"

"Lots of the three-letter agencies. I don't believe they'd do it without including FASS. So, Houck's been frozen out, he's lying, or it's an outside organization. Call him. See what he's willing to admit to."

He didn't pay attention to her as she made the call, focused on the road ahead. First option would be to duck and hide, but they'd been tracked, and vanishing wasn't a possibility. Neither of them had a weapon, and they were outnumbered. He considered the idea of finding a nearby cop shop, but that carried its own risk.

"Houck claims he doesn't know who might be following us," Harmony said softly, interrupting Jake's train of thought. "He wants us to wait for him somewhere."

"If these are bad guys, that leaves us as sitting ducks."

"How fast is your car?"

Jake liked where she was headed. "Faster than it looks. And the computer overrides have been disabled, giving me complete control. If we get to the interstate, not only can I identify how many followers we have, chances are I can outmaneuver and outrun them."

"I trust you, Jake."

He'd needed to hear that. "We'll head back to Oak Grove. We know who our friends are there."

Chapter 18

Jake was out of tricks. He didn't have the time, or a trusted dealer he could reach to swap vehicles again. The only thing he could figure out was that he and Harmony had missed the tracker when they searched his car.

Out of habit, he made the turn onto the interstate ramp at the last possible moment. The black car following them was far enough behind that it didn't have a problem tailing him. With a stroke of luck, Jake caught a break in the traffic and merged in easily while his tail got held up by several semis. Breathing room, nothing more.

After switching lanes, he glanced over to see Harmony clutching her phone. "Are you still talking to Houck?"

"No. I wanted to keep the line open. Do you need me to call him back?"

"Call your friend instead? Maybe she can find out if it's the Feds in pursuit."

"She works on the analytical side of things and not the day-to-day operations. I wonder if Freddie has picked up any chatter."

"It's worth a shot." Jake kept his eye on a black car in the left lane, but it was a different model. Half the cars surrounding them were black, making things harder.

"Freddie," Harmony said. "You're on speaker. I need some information."

"Where are you? Your car is gone, no one answered the door, and Houck isn't anywhere to be found."

"Jake and I went to lunch. Houck got lost. Forget that—is there any gossip about a federal agency running an operation between Cranberry Township and Oak Grove?"

"The office has been quiet today," Thomason's voice sounded muffled. "Too quiet."

Jake imagined Thomason resting his head on his desk.

"No, I'm not aware of anything," the detective continued. "Are you in danger? Do I need to request help from the Highway Patrol?"

"I don't have a good answer," Jake said. "So far, it could be a coincidence that I'm seeing the same model of car too many times."

"Or something more."

"Exactly," Harmony said. "You know how I feel about coincidences. We checked with Agent Houck, and he claims it has nothing to do with him or his agency."

Jake eased into the next lane, where a break in traffic gave him more room to maneuver. A black sedan filled in the spot he'd emptied but hung a car's length behind. "Angel," he said. "Can you get a look at the car to our right?"

"What's wrong?" Thomason asked.

"Nothing, yet," Jake answered.

She twisted around. "Newer model, four-door, black. Dark tint on the windows, two people in the front seat. Can't tell you about the back."

"Any markings?" asked the detective.

"Not that I can see from this angle."

"I'll change that." Jake eased off the accelerator and they dropped back until the cars were side-by-side. He held the car in that position for a few seconds and then dropped back further so the rear was visible.

"Nothing," Harmony reported. "No logos, no extra wires, not even the car company's nameplate."

"It's been modified," Thomason said. "Can you read the plate?"

"QRS . . ."

Jake swung the car sharply to the left. Harmony caught her breath, but that was all. It made him proud.

"Harmony?" Thomason asked.

"Sorry, I had to make an unexpected course correction." Jake adjusted the speed to stick close to the black car in front of them.

"There's two of them. Jake made sure we wouldn't be blocked in," Harmony explained.

She glanced at Jake for validation, and he nodded.

"Same make, same model?"

"Even the same plate series. QRS-3456. PA. Is that normal?"

"Fleet vehicle. I'll run it and verify the owner." Thomason's side of the connection switched to that peculiar dead space when the call was still active, but nobody was there.

Then he returned. "That ID isn't showing up in the system."

"Counterfeit?" Jake asked.

"It's been mentioned in our briefings, but no local cases. They've traced one fake to a dealership in New York, but that was a friend of a friend setup."

Jake gripped the steering wheel. "What the hell does that have to do with Harmony?"

"Or you," Thomason reminded him.

"Because I'm Oak Grove's favorite villain?"

"Because you're the one who's been attacked."

"Again and again," Jake murmured.

"Jake." Harmony put her hand on his knee. "Behind us."

He looked in the rearview mirror. "Shit."

"What?" Thomason demanded.

"Another one. Can't talk. There's business to take care of."

One was just a friendly competition. Two was a challenge. Three? Jake had his doubts. If these drivers knew what they were doing, he was in trouble.

A swift jerk of the steering wheel put him in the fast lane between a red semi and a chartreuse minivan. Not the ideal placement, but it gave him time to assess the setup. A white two-door economy car pulled into the spot he'd emptied, but Jake didn't expect it to stay there.

This stretch of road didn't have any left-hand exits. It did have a broad shoulder and a flat grass median his upgraded shocks should be able to handle if he needed a fast escape.

"One car pulled in behind the semi," Harmony said. "That's not logical."

"Neither was me coming over here. I should have headed towards the next exit. I confused them."

"The other two are in the lane farthest to the right."

"Blocking my access to an exit or being prepared to follow me if I evade them."

The white car disappeared from Jake's peripheral vision. The minivan braked, signaled, and switched into the spot. He sped up to close the gap to the next vehicle, an older black car with Wyoming plates.

"Give me an update," Thomason demanded.

"I don't understand," Harmony answered. "Quite the coincidence. Apparently, we just happen to be heading the same direction. They haven't made any aggressive moves."

Jake glanced her way and grinned. She'd said it with a straight face. "Harmony is right. It's like they want us to realize they are here, and nothing more."

"Highway Patrol has sent out a fake speed trap alert for twenty miles north of Cranberry to several of the GPS providers. It should show up soon. They've got a car on the way to the exit south of it, if you can hold on that far."

Fifteen miles, more or less. Unless there was a drastic change in the behavior of their followers in the next few minutes, it was doable. "Thanks for the assist. Now if we could figure out what they want."

"If HP stops one of them, we'll ask."

Jake's watch beeped. "Speed trap ahead," reported a robotic woman's voice.

"That was fast," Harmony said. "And we aren't the only ones who got it,"

Brake lights flashed in half the vehicles in front of them, but the driver from Wyoming sped up.

"What does he know that we don't?" Jake asked.

"Never mind him. Check out our tails." Harmony tapped on the side window.

Jake looked over but didn't spot the black cars. The grill of the semi filled most of the rear-view mirror. "Where did they go?"

"They dropped back right about the time we passed the sign for the next exit."

❄ ❄ ❄

"All I can figure is that they were worried about the speed trap." Thomason put another spoonful of fried rice on his plate. "They didn't want the phony plates to get identified by the detection system."

"Or it was coincidental, and they just happened to be going the same way as you were," Houck said.

With a forkful of lo mein raised to his mouth, Jake waited.

Harmony rolled her eyes. "I can't believe you said that."

The four of them were sitting around the kitchen table at Harmony's house. Thomason had suggested a debriefing of sorts and insisted on including Houck. Harmony had reluctantly agreed to allow him to eat supper with them. At least Houck had sprung for the food.

"You know I don't believe in coincidence, Doan."

She must have forgiven the agent, since she'd returned to calling him by his given name, Jake thought.

Thomason nodded. "She's right. We can't make any assumptions. Without evidence, I'm not willing to say if Jake or Harmony was the target."

"It bothers me that nothing happened until Jake switched cars." Harmony toyed with the broccoli spears on her plate, poking them with her chopsticks. "We checked it as much as we could."

"We received a new scanner at the station," Thomason said. "New to us, anyway. Chicago got the latest equipment and passed it down. I've been looking for a reason to test it. We can try it out on your car, Jake."

"Only you, Thomason. And I get a turn." Jake grinned. "I hear the newest version has bugs the makers are trying to fix. In this case, you might be better off with the older model."

"I'll set things up for tomorrow if you're free."

"Unless several miracles happen and I get permits to start repairs, my schedule is open."

Thomason chuckled. "I'll give you a buzz. In the meantime, I want to do some digging into Manny and his business."

"You think he has ties to the counterfeiters?" Harmony asked.

"I doubt he's a major player, but it wouldn't be unheard of for someone like him doing a favor for a friend of a friend."

"You have no jurisdiction outside of Oak Grove," Houck said.

It was Thomason's turn to roll his eyes. "Oak Grove isn't so isolated that I don't have contact with LEOs in nearby towns. Hell, we've even worked cases together."

He turned to Jake. "You want your name left out of it?"

"You can try." Jake curled up one side of his mouth. "Manny plays dumb, but he's smarter than most people realize. He'll make the connection between Oak Grove and me, then stick the info in his back pocket until he needs a favor."

Houck shifted in his chair. "Blackmail."

"Oh, nothing illegal. Manny knows which junkyard has the parts needed for a repair job, and I can tell him who has the specialty booze in stock for a party." Nothing as simple as that, but Jake wasn't about to share his secrets with Houck.

"Speaking of trading favors, have you had any luck getting those files?" Harmony asked Houck. "Today was aimed at Jake again, not me. I'm still not seeing anything that justifies your concerns."

"You can't be sure of that," the agent said.

"Nope, going on my gut. Freddie, are the local guys having any luck tracking down any rumors?"

"Nothing."

She laid her chopsticks across her plate. "The library board meets tomorrow to give final approval for my position. Janine isn't aware of any opposition, and it's funded by a grant, so it should be painless. Once that's settled, I'll start house-hunting."

"Are you going to sell this place?" Jake eyed the almost-empty box of sweet-n-sour chicken, but decided he'd had enough.

"Why? Do you want to buy it?"

"It doesn't require enough changes to make it worth my while. Eli talked about using it as a retreat for employees and I didn't know how involved you want to be with the company's management."

"I haven't decided yet."

"Can we get back to business?" Houck interrupted. "Your plans mean nothing if you're dead."

Harmony suddenly pushed away from the table. Her chair legs screeched on the floor. She stood and supported herself by placing both hands on the top. "There were times in the past two years, Agent Houck, when I wished I was dead. How dare you use that threat against me when I finally want to live again. Get. Out. Now."

Chapter 19

Jake was on his feet before Harmony finished speaking. Thomason was right behind him.

"You heard the lady," Jake said in a deep voice, clenching his fists.

"She's clearly unstable." Houck stood and turned to Thomason. "You can see that, right? She should be under the care of a mental health professional."

Jake didn't like where the conversation was going. The accusation could end up with Harmony held against her will and diagnosed by doctors who knew nothing about her. He wouldn't allow that to happen, even if it meant he'd go back to prison for the rest of his life.

"Where did you get your degree in psychology, Houck? Because the training you receive in the academy is inadequate and you are certainly not qualified to make a diagnosis." Thomason took a step towards the agent. "What's your agenda? It's not as simple as protecting Harmony."

"That information is on a need-to-know basis, Detective. And you have neither the need nor the credentials to gain access to the information."

"I have the clout." Harmony stood straight, her shoulders squared. "Perhaps it's more correct to say I have friends with the clout. Like Manny the Car King, we've traded favor for favor. If you want to be successful, Agent, you'd better figure that out."

Jake stared at the fire and sipped on his whiskey. He'd offered some to Harmony, but she'd turned him down and was closeted in her room with a cup of tea. They were waiting for Thomason to show up with a scanner from the police department to check if Houck had installed any new listening devices, not trusting the tools they'd already used. Harmony hadn't wanted to wait until morning.

A log in the fireplace popped, and he opened his eyes to her in the other chair, reading. He hadn't meant to fall asleep. "Did I miss anything?"

She looked up from her book. "If you're asking if Freddie has shown up, the answer is no. If you want to know if I've learned something new, it's a yes. Do you want the good news or the bad?"

After a day like this, how much worse could it be? "Let's start with the bad," Jake said.

"I researched what would happen if Agent Houck manages to have me committed for observation."

"That sounds like it deserves another shot." Jake reached for the fifth of whiskey on the side table.

"You drink too much."

"You aren't the first person to tell me that." Still, he screwed the cap back on, shoved the bottle away, and waited for her reaction. It never happened.

"Here's the deal," she continued. "I haven't given power of medical attorney to anyone. The company has its attorneys, of course, but that doesn't cover me for medical decisions."

"Oh?" Jake had no idea where this line of thought was going.

"So, if Houck had me sectioned for observation, and if he found a doctor willing to commit me, and they didn't find any living relatives, he could get a judge to appoint a guardian."

He began to see the deep pit. "And if a judge was influenced by the government to appoint a guardian that didn't have your best interests at heart…"

She nodded. "Not only could they take over medical decisions, but personal and financial ones as well."

"Giving the government control of Shifter Technologies."

"Exactly. Can you imagine the damage?"

"How do you fix it?"

"Ask a friend for a favor. Someone I can rely on."

"Sarah? Janine?"

"You."

Jake reached for the bottle but stopped himself. "You trust me that much?"

"Sarah and Janine have lived in Oak Grove most of their lives. They don't see the bigger picture. You look at things a different way, examine a problem from many angles. That's what I need in a personal representative."

"Even with your money?"

She quirked her mouth. "I will get my lawyers to write the agreement up with so much oversight you'll need to fight for every penny. It can be done."

"Trust but verify?"

"I'll give you the night to consider it."

He shook his head. "I can answer right now. For you, Angel, anything."

"Thank you. I've pulled a generic form off the internet. We'll get Freddie to witness it and have it as a safeguard until the lawyers draw one up."

"What makes you think he'll agree? Besides, don't you need two witnesses?"

She ran a finger over the lip of her teacup. "Freddie will take some persuading, but he'll break down and do it. I'll ask Agent Houck to be the other one."

Was she crazy? Jake turned to see her lips quivering as she struggled to maintain a straight face. He relaxed. "You had me there."

"I don't know if he'd have a heart attack or call for backup to take me in."

"And I don't want to find out."

❋ ❋ ❋

Jake retreated to his room on the third floor as soon as Thomason pulled up in front of the house. He wanted to be no part of the conversation. "Conversation" was the polite way to put it, because the sound of yelling traveled up to where he stood, staring out the picture window. The noise stopped, to be replaced by the creaking of stairs.

When he spotted the detective's reflection in the glass, Jake raised his hands shoulder-high. "Don't shoot. It wasn't my idea. I tried to talk her out of it."

Thomason snorted. "Put your hands down and pour me a glass of something strong, will you? I caved in to her crazy scheme and I'm regretting it already."

"I don't have my usual assortment to pick from, but I'll do what I can." Jake poured a shot into a tumbler for Thomason and handed it to him, then repeated the action for himself.

"The longer I think about it, the more I agree with her. It's not paranoia if someone is really out to get you." Jake continued.

"Which is why you've amazed me this past week. If anyone has a reason to be paranoid, it's you," Thomason said.

Jake tossed the rest of his drink down in one swallow. "Downstairs," he said. "We have to include Harmony."

In the living room, Jake picked up the remote for the scrambling device and turned it on. "What you said upstairs, that I'm not paranoid, triggered a thought. I've been busy trying to figure out what the attacks on me have to do with the threat against Harmony."

Harmony nodded and Thomason said, "Right."

"So, what if we're looking at it backwards?"

"Backwards?" Harmony asked.

"Anyone could figure out I'd do anything for you, Angel." Jake stared into the mirror above the fireplace and watched their reflections. "What if someone figured this would be the perfect opportunity to use you against me?"

"What are you talking about, Jake? I would never hurt you."

He started pacing. "Not on purpose. Do you remember a long time ago when the FBI blackmailed me to go undercover with a suspected moonshine ring?"

"I remember." She started pacing as well, going the opposite direction, her cane thumping with each step.

"Was that when they ended up busting a gun running operation?" Thomason asked. "What's that got to do with now?"

"Same principle." Jake stopped in his tracks. "They— whoever they are—have me scrambling, wondering when the next disaster will hit. If Harmony disappears and I have to agree to work with someone—say the counterfeiters—to get her back, don't you think I'd do it in a heartbeat?"

Harmony stopped on the other side of the room. "You're at a disadvantage because you don't know who to trust and would have to go it alone."

Without my normal resources. "Right. And I'm expendable. If I die trying, it's no big loss. That may be what they are hoping for."

"They had their chance today." Thomason pointed out.

"Until you called in backup. That wasn't part of the plan." Jake rubbed his wrist below his cast..

"Who do you think 'they' are?"

"That's the question. From what Houck says, FASS doesn't have the resources, and it's not a job they'd handle, anyway. The FBI does, and Houck collaborated with the FBI on the day of Sorenson's funeral. That makes them a candidate."

Thomason shook his head. "Issues with license plates are state level, unless the mail is used to get them to their destination. Then the postal inspectors get involved. Although it's logical to think this has something to do with the fake plates, it's possible it's something else."

"There's one thing I can't wrap my head around. Why not just ask me for help?" Jake asked.

"Because they want you to do something illegal. No one has been able to pin any crimes on you no matter how hard they've tried, so they are manufacturing the opportunity and forcing you into it. Imagine the ego boost for the LEO that pulls that off."

"It's a good starting point." Harmony resumed pacing, her limp more pronounced. "I'll get my contact with DHS to see if she can identify any inter-agency investigations locally. I'll also ask her to get a copy of Houck's personnel file so I can see how his current assignment reads."

"You have a friend in the Department of Homeland Security?" Thomason asked.

"Worse." She stopped in front of the detective and leaned on her cane. "She's in the Office of Intelligence and Analysis. Way up in the chain of command as these things go."

"You trust her?"

"She was my roommate once upon a time and we've stayed in contact. I helped her get a promotion back then." Harmony grinned. "She still owes me. So, until I can reach out to her, what's the plan?"

Jake turned to face the fireplace, holding his hands out towards the dwindling fire. He didn't want her to read his expression. "Above all else, we need to protect you, Angel. Easiest way to accomplish that is for you to get far away from here. You have the money you need to go anywhere you want. Where do you want to start?"

"Here. I want to start here and stay here."

"Jake is right. It isn't safe for you here," Thomason said.

"Deal with it. I'm not leaving. Consider this: Houck has been trying to get me to return to Orlando since I got here. How does that fit in?"

Jake swiveled. "It doesn't. The whole theory falls apart."

"Are the settings right on that scanner?" Jake asked, exasperated. Every room he and Thomason scanned had reported an active tag, but they'd been unable to locate any of them. "We checked a few days ago, and the house came up clean."

"I'll try again, but I downloaded a fresh copy of the manual." Thomason wiggled a knob on the device that reminded Jake of a hand-held vacuum cleaner. The machine beeped and the test light flashed red.

Jake frowned. "The only thing I can come up with is that Harmony's scanner is outdated, and the bugs are a new technology. It just kills me that Houck has been listening in on our conversations."

"Grab it and run a test in here."

"Here" being the spare bedroom on the second floor that Houck had occupied. Jake wasn't sure he understood the logic of placing a bug in it, since it was currently unoccupied. "I'll be right back."

He got as far as the top of the staircase when Thomason yelled.

"Jake. Come back."

"What? Is my electric personality setting it off?" Jake joked.

"Stop outside the door."

"Are we playing a game?"

Thomason stood by the window on the far side of the room and squeezed the trigger. Nothing happened. Two steps closer, and still no response from the scanner. The detective waited until he was halfway across the room and received a faint ping.

"What the hell?" Jake asked.

Thomason closed the gap between them and ran another test. The machine beeped loudly.

Jake swore. "Shit. That can't be right."

"Take off your watch. Maybe it's causing a false positive," the detective suggested.

Jake took it, his phone, and his belt off and left them in the bathroom. "Try again," he said when he returned to the doorway.

The lights flashed an angry red. "Strip. Down to your briefs."

Jake had his shirt off before he reached the bathroom.

Everything else followed. "Try it while I'm here," he suggested.

The machine remained silent, and the light flashed green when Thomason ran the test. "Can it be attached to the hem of your jeans?" he suggested.

A tag would be easy to find if that were true, but he'd washed the pants two days ago. "Let's run one more test." Jake walked down the hall and stood in front of Thomason.

"Do it." he said. The light flashed red. He reached for the waistband of his underwear, although he couldn't figure out how they could hide a bug.

Thomason shook his head. "Don't bother. I know where it is." He grabbed Jake's left wrist.

Chapter 20

Shirtless, Jake propped his left arm on the kitchen table while Thomason picked at the side of his cast with a paring knife.

"I spotted it glinting in the overhead light when you walked towards me. It's in a place where you'd never see it." Thomason carefully stabbed the plaster.

"I just got this cast. I can't believe the doc is in on this."

"Did Doc Gabe set the cast personally?"

"No, Trina handles that. Of course, she's on her annual fall vacation and they have a tech come from Pittsburgh to cover her. She goes to Florida to meet up with old friends and recreate spring break without the hassle of the crowds."

Thomason stared at Jake.

It took a heartbeat until the realization hit him.

"Shit."

Thomason nodded. "I'll handle that investigation. And here it is," he said, holding up a small metallic object the size of a pushpin. "I'm pretty sure I destroyed it in the removal process, but we should whack it with a hammer or something."

"We can use that handy-dandy butcher block behind you." Jake wiggled the fingers of his left hand, realizing he'd been clenching his fist while the detective worked. "Or should we let Harmony do it?"

"I wasn't going to tell her." Thomason shrugged. "Protecting her, you know. But you're right, we shouldn't keep secrets from her."

It was almost as fun watching Harmony beat the device into submission as doing it himself. Almost. She'd also taken the time to examine the tag under a magnifying glass to look for identifying marks, which Jake hadn't thought about. There weren't any, but he admired her meticulous attempt.

She dumped the pieces into the garbage, closed the bag, and handed it to Thomason. "Get it out of here. Don't even toss this in my bin. Mr. Haggerty leaves his container at the end of his driveway. Use it."

Thomason grinned and gave her a half-salute. "Yes. Ma'am."

She waited until Thomason was out the door before she turned to Jake. "You. Go put on a shirt."

"You've seen it before," Jake reminded her.

"You've gotten a new tattoo since then."

"Several of them. The cast covers one." He didn't mention it was a tribute to Eli. "I keep them small so I can maintain my cover as a businessman."

"Is that all it is? A cover for your other pursuits?"

How much does she know? "It surprises even me, some days, the way I enjoy running the bars. And the contracting gig is a bonus. I like fixing up houses."

"You're avoiding the question."

"What answer are you looking for, Angel?" he asked, locking his eyes to hers. He longed to wrap his arms around her, but she remained forbidden territory.

"I got a file from my contact about local people who are potential security risks. You had a whole section devoted to your suspected but unproven crimes. I was impressed."

"The key word is 'unproven'. Law enforcement has a habit of throwing things at me and seeing what sticks. Nothing ever does. That doesn't stop them from trying again."

She reached up and touched his cheek. "And you love watching them fail."

His smile was lopsided. "It gives me a certain satisfaction."

Her hand dropped, and he missed her touch.

"A note in the file caught my eye," she said.

"Oh?" Jake had no idea where she was headed. With Harmony, that could be dangerous.

"It was a name. Two names, really. Ashleigh and Amanda Zabrowski. Mother and daughter, apparently. Followed by a line of question marks. Does that ring any bells?"

"Ashleigh Zabrowski?" Jake repeated, stalling for time.

"Ashliegh Zabrowski. Isn't she the lady who disappeared a few years ago?" Thomason asked as he walked back into the kitchen. "Sorry to interrupt, but that was an interesting case. Her boyfriend reported her missing. He had a file a mile long that included reports of domestic violence. We tried to connect the dots, wondering if he'd killed her, but he had an airtight alibi. Besides, a few personal items were gone, including the kid's favorite toys. We figured she went into hiding."

"Didn't she pop up somewhere a few months later?" Jake asked, knowing the answer.

"Yeah. A small town in Oregon. That happened after the arrest of the boyfriend for a string of charges after a fight in a bar."

"Not mine, thankfully, although I got questioned because he'd been a customer on a few occasions. Wasn't that up in Erie?"

Thomason nodded. "Yep. Saved us a lot of work."

"Did she just get into her car and leave?" Harmony asked.

She isn't going to let it go. Jake was in trouble.

"No car. Best we could figure," Thomason said, "was that a friend talked her into leaving. Or someone from the shelter, although officially, they had no record of her. It made me happy that it worked out in the end, no matter how."

Thomason picked up the scanner. "It's good to get a win once in a while. Even small victories help. Like tonight. Still, I want to make one more walk-through and make sure the bug in the cast wasn't masking anything else."

"I'll come along," Jake said. "To see how the scanner works normally." Actually, he wanted to get away from

Harmony. She would ask questions he didn't want to answer.

He waited until she was tucked away for the night to descend from his third-floor room and take up his watchdog duties. There wasn't a tale he could weave that she'd believe. By morning, she might face a new challenge to distract her.

After making sure the fire was out and the fireplace screen closed, Jake settled into an easy chair, a glass of water handy on the coffee table. He wouldn't drink any, but he wanted to impress Harmony. Twenty-two years hadn't cured him

The picture was completed with a biography of a woman Jake had never heard of who had been involved with the beginnings of the computer industry. He dozed off quickly, even without the help from his normal nighttime shot of booze.

"Wake up, Jake."

He wasn't ready for this conversation and kept his eyes closed. "Go back to bed, Angel, unless it's important."

"You said you can hide me if I want to disappear. That it would be more secure than a government safe house."

He sighed, opened his eyes, and sat up. "I did."

"I thought you were bragging. Inflating yourself to put Agent Houck in his place."

"That may have played into my motivation."

"How many women have you helped?"

"Don't fool yourself into thinking I'm some kind of hero. I'm not." Jake reached for the nonexistent glass of whiskey and picked up the water instead. The warm liquid trickling down his throat did nothing to ease the tension.

"When was the last time you stole a piece of jewelry?"

"You won't like the answer."

"According to the file, it was five years ago, at a wedding in Cleveland. The day the theft was reported, you were here in Oak Grove and attended a City Council meeting that night."

Jake chuckled. "That would have been Agent Young of the FBI. My lawyer said the item—a gold necklace—showed up at a pawnshop in Pittsburgh and he tried to get me on a charge of trafficking stolen goods across state lines."

"You were here."

"One of the agenda items was decommissioning the traffic meters along Main Street. Figures showed they cost more to maintain than they brought in in revenue. It didn't affect the bar, but I came as moral support for a friend who wanted to speak and is shy."

Based on the pictures he'd seen, the necklace wasn't worth the effort to steal it, anyway. Besides, it went against Jake's ethics to carry out a heist on his home turf, and Cleveland counted as a second home.

Harmony's eyes narrowed. "Then how did you get accused?"

"There was a good reason. The man who pawned the necklace resembled a younger me. He was several inches shorter and didn't have my tattoos. Should have been a dead giveaway, but Young was determined to pin it on me."

"Could he be behind this?"

❋ ❋ ❋

"My contact in the Pittsburgh office says Young is assigned to a New Hampshire office and doing well. That's all he'd share." Thomason had brought the news, along with a bouquet from Sarah, when he stopped by mid-morning. He and Jake were in the front room while Harmony had taken the flowers to the kitchen to find a vase and get them into water.

"Seems like an unlikely prospect for our villain," Jake said. "Back to the drawing board."

"It was worth the shot, but I'm stuck on the idea that whoever is responsible is local—or at least has local connections. Especially since I've been ordered to back off and let Houck do his job."

"That's why Sarah got the notion to send Harmony flowers and for you to deliver them. Was it Houck's request to cut you out? Or his boss's? Or someone hoping he'll keep chasing bad info?"

Thomason shrugged. "I don't have the pull to get that information."

"Eli did. I'm willing to bet Harmony does too, if she stops to think about it. After all, Eli's company developed the software the police department uses. At least, I'm guessing it hasn't changed."

"The request would never be put in the records."

Thomason shook his head. "It would be done verbally. Two officers chatting over coffee or waiting for their cars to charge before hitting the streets."

"I guess nothing comes easy. It would have been fun to see what Harmony could find."

"Now that you mention it, there's been some talk that we need a new system. A few of the patrolmen have been talking about how great the programs they used in their former jobs were. I haven't paid any attention, because those decisions all come from up the chain of command."

"Would anyone besides you be able to make the connection between Harmony and the software?"

"Sure. Sometimes, when Eli and Harmony visited Oak Grove, they'd have lunch with Sorenson. Eli talked with whoever was in the office to see what problems they had. They just called him 'that computer guy,' and I don't think they realized he owned the company. Where are you headed with this?"

"Poaching. Stealing customers. Hostile takeover." Harmony stood in the doorway to the kitchen, the vase of flowers in her hands. "Well, not so much the last one since the company isn't publicly owned."

She limped over and put the vase on the coffee table, eyed the placement, and moved it an inch. "It would be a hard sell to replace our software based on price point alone, but if officials were convinced the owner is a security risk, it could be done."

"Meaning you?" Jake asked.

"Meaning me."

"And the fastest way to do that…?"

She moved the vase half an inch back. "Is to get you involved in something illegal and then tie the two of us together."

"They've already accomplished the second part." Not in the way Jake wished, but still, he was living in her house.

"And tried the first part by torching the bar," Thomason said. "Which didn't work, because the report came through from the fire investigator and you're in the clear. They found evidence to link the accelerant and method used to a known arsonist. He's under arrest and being questioned."

"They'll try to connect him to me."

"It would be a tough sell. Especially as the locals aren't in charge of the questioning."

"We should celebrate with a drink!"

Harmony coughed.

"Too early?" Jake asked.

"I'm on duty," Thomason said.

"True. Still, I'll take the win. But all of this is speculation."

The detective shrugged. "It's the best theory we've come up with. How do we prove it?"

Chapter 21

The waiting room of the city offices was empty, but—with a nod to Alice, the receptionist—, Jake made a show of grabbing a number from the ticket dispenser for his turn. It was a standing joke between them after a council member took offense that the numbers weren't being used up quickly enough, and that would mean customers were being served out of order. After the councilman accepted the invitation to sit and watch the traffic flow for a few hours—on a slow day—the complaining had ceased.

Alice grinned widely. "Serving customer—what number do you have, Mr. Hennessey?"

He leaned on the counter and flashed his award-winning smile. "Thirty-two. It must be a busy day."

She giggled. Alice was fresh out of high school, so Jake had to tone down his normal level of flirting to friendly banter. It was an art form he'd perfected. He didn't want to become a creepy old man.

"It's Wednesday. That's the entire week." She giggled again. "It gave me the time to work ahead on my classes."

"Still hoping for a degree in public administration? Even after working here?"

"They let me sit in on a discussion about putting out a bid for garbage pickup."

"The company we have now has been slacking," Jake said.

"Yeah, we receive lots of complaints. Started when they were bought out. City Council wants to find other companies interested in providing the service."

"Any other contracts up for proposals? Like for the street lights or police department?" Alice was in a perfect position to hear the news before it became official.

She ran her hand across her short, purple hair. "Chief Santos has been spending time talking to Jim, but all the department heads are. It's budget planning time."

Jim Nyugen was the city manager. The meetings proved nothing.

"Anyway, who are you here to see?" Alice asked.

"Anyone in the planning department. I want to check on any new city codes I have to account for when drawing up the plans for repairing the bar."

She checked the computer. "Cecil Rogers is available. He'll help you out."

❊ ❊ ❊

"I didn't realize how much everyone has been avoiding me." Thomason was reporting on his research by phone. He'd decided to limit the time he spent with Jake and Harmony—at least to the casual observer. "People stop talking when I walk into a room, that sort of thing. It became painfully obvious by the end of the day."

"So, no one is discussing changes down at the shop?" Harmony asked. Jake had provided supper with a stopover at the Dairy Barn. They sat in the living room, taking advantage of Eli's masking system, just in case.

"Nothing. The juiciest gossip I overheard was about Santos hiring another new patrolman and wondering who was leaving."

"He's getting rid of the old officers and replacing them with his hand-picked minions. When will it be your turn, Thomason?" Jake asked.

Dead air was the response. Jake didn't know if the call had dropped or if he'd hung up.

"Freddie?" Harmony asked. "Freddie?"

"Sorry," he said. "I moved out to the garage. I don't want to worry Sarah."

"That bad?"

"Based on my reputation, contacts, and experience, I've got pull that Santos doesn't, and it bothers him. He'd like to get rid of me. I'm a year from full retirement, and there have been rumors about a lawsuit based on age discrimination from some of the older officers. He'll assign me to desk duty and make my last year as miserable as possible."

Thomason chuckled. "He forgot about the Harmony effect. I'm pretty sure that when he assigned me to work as Houck's liaison, he thought I'd fade into the woodwork. But nothing is ever simple with you, Harmony. You're the only person I know who could turn a funeral into a terrorist threat and crime spree. If I can get to the bottom of everything, I'll be untouchable until I decide I'm ready to retire."

When it came to Harmony, everyone had an agenda, Jake thought. *Including me.* Or was his more of a pipe dream?

"I had no luck at City Hall, either," Jake said. "Place was too quiet. The top dogs had gone to a conference, so half the staff took the day off. How about you, Angel?"

"I expect it to take a few days." She dipped her spoon into her soup and let the liquid drain back into the bowl. "I may have downplayed the issue, so Lando and Scotty wouldn't feel the need to come and rescue me."

"How do you do it, Thomason?" Jake asked. "I know investigations drag on—I've been on the other side a few times—but I hoped we'd figure something out quickly."

"I live with frustration. After a while, you get used to it."

❄ ❄ ❄

"Has Houck stopped by today?" Jake took a cup from the sink and placed it in the dishwasher while Harmony wiped down the kitchen table. It meant nothing more than him and Danny washing up after the bar closed, he reminded himself.

"He came over for his daily check-in while you were downtown and we had our normal chat about his progress." Harmony rolled her eyes. "I made him sit on the porch so he couldn't plant more of his listening devices."

"Which means he knows nothing new and hasn't received any files from his higher-ups. He's consistent if nothing else. What about your friend at DHS?"

"She's reviewing the document that FASS intrepreted as a threat. The conclusions she's drawing are different than those of the original analyst. Until she completes her work, she won't share it."

"So, there's no danger to you?"

"She didn't say that. Wouldn't say that when I pressured her. Makes me wonder if there is an implied threat, but coming from a different source."

Jake closed the dishwasher with too much force. "Did she tell Houck?"

"No, and neither will we until we have better intel." She limped over to the counter with the salt and pepper shakers in her hand, her back turned towards him.

Jake took the container of salt away from her, then put his hand under her chin and guided her face to his. "What are you hiding from me, Angel?"

"She asked if there had been any major changes lately in the policies and procedures for the company. There haven't been, but I need to get Lando and Scotty to assign it as a project to someone. The question is, if she brought it up, does that mean she thinks an employee is involved?" Harmony supported herself with one hand on the counter.

Ignoring his baser inclinations, Jake wrapped his arms around her in a loose, supportive hug. "You're borrowing trouble. I'm sure your friend is covering every possibility. But you know who might help?"

She looked up, and he wiped a tear away. "Houck. He worked the help desk. Don't they hear all the rumors?"

Houck eyed the chocolate cake that Harmony placed on the kitchen table in front of him. "Are you trying to bribe me?"

"I don't imagine you bribe easily, Doan." Harmony fluttered her eyelashes. "Or at all. Call it a peace offering."

"You want something." Houck picked up his fork. "What?"

"Your impressions about your time on the help desk."

He stopped with the forkful of cake halfway to his mouth. "Excuse me?"

"It's time for me to be re-involved in the running of the business. As much as I trust my executive team, it'll be good to have an outsider's impression of general management. So, how was it going?"

"Aren't there consultants you could hire?"

"Of course." Harmony nodded. "And none of them would get the inside scoop. Like, how hard is it for a help desk tech to advance to another role in the company? And how are they treated by the customers?"

Jake turned away and smiled. Houck had no idea of how long of a night he was in for. Jake had seen Harmony in action and was glad he wasn't in the hot seat. He filled a pitcher with ice water and set it and two glasses on the table. Then he picked up his cake and headed for the third floor. The agent would reveal more without Jake's presence.

Around the hour mark, Jake decided enough was enough. It wasn't a police interrogation, wearing down a suspect to get the answers the cops wanted, and it had gone on long enough that he doubted Harmony was getting any additional useful information.

He clomped down the stairs, hitting every squeaky spot he'd found. He had them mapped in his head just like he had every street and alley in Oak Grove memorized. The agent was putting the plates in the dishwasher when Jake entered the kitchen, while Harmony still sat at the table instead of helping, a rarity for her.

"Jake, would you find a leftover container for Doan, please? I promised him a piece of cake in case he gets the munchies in the middle of the night."

Jake rummaged through the cupboards. "How's the heating in the house over there? Staying warm enough? If the place ever goes on the market, I'll be able to factor that into my offer."

"I suppose you'd like a tour," Houck said.

"Yes, but not tonight. Will this work?" Jake pulled a white container off a shelf. He could get into the house any time he wanted, but he was playing by the rules.

"That'll do fine. There's plastic silverware in the drawer." Harmony sounded tired. Was she pushing herself too hard?

Jake grabbed a few napkins, piled everything into a neat stack, and handed them to Houck. "I'll walk you out."

They stood on the porch and watched a police car drive by. The streetlights were on, but it was dark, and Jake couldn't identify which officer was driving. A light breeze barely ruffled the few leaves remaining on the bushes that lined the sidewalk.

"She's a smart woman," Houck said. "I didn't realize how smart. I mean, I'd heard stories, but it seemed like Mr. Hennessey was the one who got all the glory. She pulled information out of me I didn't realize I knew."

"Because she wanted it that way. They were equals, but she didn't like the limelight. The two of them were made for each other."

"And you resent that."

"I was responsible for them getting together."

"And how did you meet her?"

"Coincidence, Agent Houck. I was just fate's way of arranging for them to meet. I'm a victim of the universe."

"It appears the universe doesn't like you very much."

Or I've used up all my good will. Jake shook his head. "It seems that way. I need to figure out how to get back on the universe's good side. Should I sacrifice a bottle of fine whiskey, or what?"

Houck stepped off the porch and onto the sidewalk. "Keep your bad luck away from Mrs. Duprie."

I'm trying. "Have a good night, Agent."

Houck stopped at the end of the sidewalk and looked both ways. He tucked the container of cake under his arm and stepped off the curb. Jake raised his head to watch the flashing lights of a plane headed towards Pittsburgh. A car engine purred as it started. Jake half-expected crickets to chirp and birds to sing, but it was too late in the year for the crickets.

Houck stopped halfway across the street and bent over to look at something. At least, that's what Jake thought he was doing. The agent picked an item off the pavement and held it up to his face. From the corner of his eye, Jake caught movement at the end of the block. A car whined its way down the street, honking, and Houck turned to identify the commotion.

Jake didn't have the ability to stop time. He yelled and accomplished nothing. The car struck Houck, tossing him into the air. He landed on its roof and rolled to the ground, his head crunching on the concrete. The container of cake plopped to the ground on the sidewalk and split open. With a squeal of its tires, the car sped off and turned at the corner.

Chapter 22

Jake sat on the front steps of Harmony's house, elbows propped on his knees, and tracked the ambulance as it pulled away. It was headed to the health clinic to meet a helicopter to take Houck to Pittsburgh. No one seemed certain he'd survive the trip.

A half-dozen cop cars and an assortment of fire rescue vehicles lined the street, their various lights piercing the dark. Police tape cordoned off both ends of the block. Small crowds huddled near the intersections. Jake spotted three reporters mixed in with the locals.

He pulled a hand wipe from the package, and swiped his hands and wrists again. He'd spent a short time in handcuffs—until Harmony had shown the cops the security tapes—but that wasn't the issue. Despite having washed them four times since administering what little first aid he could to Houck while on the phone with 9-1-1, he couldn't get rid of the lingering scent of blood. It might help to change clothes, but his cast needed to be replaced.

He'd never had this issue after any of the fights he'd

been in. This was different—it had been a deliberate attempt to murder Houck.

Or me. They were nearly equal in height, and although Houck was more muscular, it would be hard to tell in the dark. Jake supposed that the cake container could fool an unobservant person into thinking it was his cast. He'd voiced his speculation to no one.

"How long will they stick around?" Harmony asked from behind him. She was sitting in a kitchen chair someone had brought outside for her.

"It's going to get worse before it gets better." Jake dropped the used wipe onto the growing pile beside him. "I figure we have fifteen minutes or so until the Feds swarm the neighborhood. That means you have ten to decide if you want to stick around or disappear."

"How hard is it to make that happen?"

"Depends on how much planning time I have. Most of the women lost their friends, family, and money because of their abuser. They had nothing left. You have everything to lose, and I've had minimal planning time."

"Except Eli. I already lost him."

"You still have friends, a job, more money than you'll ever need. If you started over, you'd lose all of that. Including the money, because the Feds would track that to locate you. Can you start over from scratch? You've never known what scratch really is."

Harmony sat silent.

"Ten minutes, Angel," Jake said.

"If I stay, how bad will it be?"

"I expect representatives from half a dozen federal

agencies to show up. I won't even guess the off-the-books numbers. But you know that better than me."

"How many women have you helped?"

More than he cared to reveal. "I'm just a link in the chain."

"After this is over, I want in."

"No matter what you decide, I may need to get out. Too many eyes watching me and I become a weak point. Five minutes." Besides, he'd compromised most of his hiding spots.

She sighed—or was that a strangled sob?

"I'm staying. Help me, Jake."

"Anything I can do, Angel, you know that. But you should get in touch with your friend at DHS—the one you never name. The distant whirr of helicopter blades whispered through the air.

"He wasn't a bad guy," Harmony said. "I hope he'll be okay."

"He never should have been assigned the case. He was in over his head. His supervisor should have recognized the need for backup."

"Hindsight."

A lone figure crossed the police line and headed in their direction. "And so it starts," Jake muttered.

"Who is it?" she asked.

"Chief Santos. Study how he holds himself. The artificial stiffness. He's trying to mimic Chief Sorenson's command presence, without the personality to carry it off. I suggest you get your lawyers on the phone before he starts to throw his weight around."

"What can he do?"

"He'll try to convince you to go downtown to give a statement. That way, when the Feds get here, they'll need his permission to talk to you. Make himself more important than he is. But he was slow to react and has lost what little lead time he had."

"What about you?" Harmony asked as she typed something into her phone.

"Me? I'll be surprised if I get as much as a hello. As far as he is concerned, I'm nothing but a nuisance."

The State Police showed up a few minutes later. Jake wondered who had the pull to make that happen in the middle of the night. Next was the FBI. A representative from the U.S. Marshals arrived to cover bodyguard services for Harmony until they assigned a new FASS agent to the case.

The street was soon lined with black sedans and delivery trucks. Jake couldn't figure out who was in charge, but there was a pattern to the chaos as equipment and furniture were hauled into the Formby house, and garbage was taken out. Santos, after doing the obligatory meet and greet, had left. He wasn't being ignored, but he hadn't been welcomed either. Jake thought that was a tactical error, but it wasn't his place to say anything. He took a few minutes to change his clothes, then returned to watch the show.

At two a.m., the deputy marshal, a man the size of a pro-football defensive lineman, finished his trip around the house and came to sit beside Jake on the porch steps. "Did Mrs. Duprie-Hennessey finally go to sleep?"

"She went to her room and turned off the lights, but I doubt the sleep part, Deputy Warren."

Warren nodded. "You might want to head home and get some rest yourself."

"I've been staying here. Kind of an early-warning system. It makes Harmony feel less vulnerable."

"The briefing I received didn't mention that. The notes were minimal, but I hope that's rectified by morning when the incident commander gets here."

"No worries. For the record, we are old friends. I use a bed on the third floor, but mostly I've been sleeping in a chair in the front room."

"Still, you should get some rest."

"I can't. There's someone missing and I can't figure it out."

Warren stretched his long legs in front of him and leaned back on his elbows. "Two people, actually. The DHS rep is on the way and there are rumors the CIA is involved. This is quite the task force."

"Oak Grove won't know how to handle the excitement." Jake had sent texts to some of the bar patrons, telling them to stay close to home and behave. "But they aren't who I'm worried about. Detective Thomason from the local police hasn't shown his face."

"I've seen any number of locals getting in the way," Warren chuckled.

"Yeah, but he's a friend of hers. Even if he wasn't assigned to the case, he'd call or something. Harmony and his wife are lifelong best friends."

The deputy frowned. "Has she reached out to him?"

"I haven't brought it up to her. She didn't need the

stress. But I texted him-three times-and got no reply. It's not like him to turn his phone off or let it go dead. I tried his wife with the same result. She and I do business together, but it's unlikely she'd answer a call from me this late at night."

"Have you asked his fellow officers?"

"Here's the issue. I don't know which ones to trust." Jake shrugged. "The department is in transition, and Detective Thomason seems to be on the wrong side as far as the chief is concerned."

"Got it. Stay here. I'll be right back."

Jake watched as the deputy dashed across the street, weaved between various delivery drivers, and entered the home that Houck had been using, now headquarters for the task force. He returned in a few minutes with a tall, middle-aged man in the classic black suit. FBI. Jake's initial impression was that he was a desk jockey, but the way he carried himself indicated a man who'd seen plenty of action. A man to keep his eye on.

"Agent Sam Matney," Warren said. "I borrowed him."

"I got roped into assembling desks. This is a welcome break," the agent said, dusting dirt off his pants. "Deputy Warren filled me in on what little he knows. Is there anything more you can tell me before I go check out the detective's house, Mr. Hennessey?"

"I'm going with you. The GPS will loop you through the round-about and take you down three streets and ask for a U-turn. I'll get you there faster," Jake said.

"You're right," Matney said, parking at the end of an

alley half a block from Thomason's ranch-style home. "The GPS would never have found this place."

"The joys of an old town."

"Which house is Thomason's?"

"The brown and tan one."

"All the lights are off."

"Which is odd. Have you ever known a cop to keep his outside lights off?" Jake asked.

"No. And the rest of the houses have electricity so, unless he didn't pay his bill, that's not the issue."

"His cruiser is missing."

"Explain."

Jake leaned forward and studied the street. "Sarah—his wife—has a car they park in the garage. It's a mini-van she uses for real-estate showings. Thomason has a small pickup for personal use. It's in the driveway. But the cops take their patrol cars home to make the town appear to have a larger force than it does. He parks it in front of his house."

"If he'd gotten called in, his porch light would be on," Matney said. "Do you carry a gun?"

Jake shook his head. "I don't. It's a personal rule. Long story."

"Then you stay here. I'll make a loop around the house to see what I can see. Do they have a dog?"

"I don't think so."

Matney reached up and hit the switch for the overhead light. When he opened his door, nothing lit up to give their presence away. He stood and buttoned his his jacket so as little of his shirt showed as possible. His brown skin blended in with the night. When he closed his door, the click was almost silent.

Jake approved. The agent was good.

Matney was back in five minutes. He got in the car, closed the door, and stared out the front window.

"Nothing," Jake guessed.

"Too much of nothing. I don't like it."

Jake didn't either. "Did you try the doors?"

"Front and back locked. And I don't have a compelling reason for a warrant."

"Heat imaging?"

"Not with me. I'm assigned to help with analyzing financial aspects of the case, if we find any."

"Nothing is simple when it comes to Harmony. Where do we go from here?"

The agent drummed his fingers on the dashboard. "I'd sure like to get into that house and check it out."

Jake was positive he could find a way in—an unlocked window, the back door having an older lock, the garage not being secure—but this felt like a trap. How far would the Feds go to put him out of business? Unless Thomason was a better actor than Jake realized, he couldn't imagine the cop being part of the conspiracy.

A police car drove past and stopped in front of Thomason's house. Perhaps one of his fellow officers checking on him?

"Do you have access to Oak Grove's secure band?" Jake asked.

"No. They haven't shared that info." Matney jerked

his head towards Thomason's house. "I assume you want to hear what's going on."

"And who's driving that car. Can you see its ID?"

The agent leaned past Jake, unlocked the glove box, and pulled out a pair of folding binoculars. "These aren't the greatest, but they work in a pinch."

He held them up to his eyes and fiddled with various dials. "Five-two-one-one. Does that mean anything to you?"

"No, I've never tried figuring out the numbering system. Normally, the newer guys get the piece of shit older vehicles." At least, that was the way it used to work. He'd spotted rookies driving shiny new cars while Thomason's had seen better days.

"I can't make out the driver's features," Matney reported. He lowered the binoculars. "The streetlight is burnt out."

Or shot out. In the past, Jake had paid teenagers to handle the "prank" for a job or two.

"Dispatch might tell us who is driving and where Thomason's car is. Maybe it's being worked on." Jake pulled his phone out of his pocket but covered the face with his hand to dim the light.

He got the message about it being the non-emergency number and to dial 9-1-1 in case of needing immediate assistance, then waited for the recording listing extensions before hitting 0. It took two rings for the line to be answered.

"City of Oak Grove, this is Aubrey. How can I direct your call?"

Jake put the phone on speaker. "Good morning, Beautiful."

"Jake Hennessey. Long time no talk. In fact, you're the last person I expected to hear from after the excitement you caused tonight. I figured you'd be in the company of our out-of-town visitors."

"I am. At least one of them. I'm with a member of the FBI."

"A pretty one?"

"No, but you might think differently. I'll introduce you. Besides, I swore off women after you broke my heart."

She snorted. "Give me a break. What do you need, Hennessey?"

"Two things, both easy. Is Detective Thomason's patrol car in the shop again?"

"Let me check." Jake heard her fingers flying across her keyboard. "Why do you want to know?"

"I thought I saw someone else driving it and was curious."

"Chances that our mechanic came in at this time of the night to work on it are slim to none." The typing stopped. "That's weird. It's not transmitting a GPS signal. At all. The only time that should happen is if the battery has been pulled during servicing."

"So, it's the mechanic, after all. How about car five-two-one-one?"

"Don't even have to look it up. That's Morrison."

"You don't sound too happy about it."

"You buy me a stiff drink after your bar reopens and I'll tell you the reasons. Not here and not now where someone can overhear."

"Got it. Thanks. I owe you."

"Big time. Tread carefully, Hennessey, whatever you're involved in."

"Always. Bye."

Jake disconnected the call. The car in front of Thomason's house hadn't moved.

"What's the story?" Matney asked.

"Aubrey? Her dad was a cop. She had a mid-life crisis after he died, got divorced, and followed in his footsteps. Even got accepted to the police academy. Started and had a medical incident a couple of days in. That's when the docs discovered a heart condition and washed her out of training. She took a job as a dispatcher as a consolation prize."

"That's rough."

"I offered her comfort when she needed it. We remain friends."

"You're an interesting person. I need to review your file and see what's not there. But you don't believe Thomason's car is in the shop, do you?"

"Not for a minute."

"Are he and Morrison on good terms?"

"I don't know, and I wasn't going to ask Aubrey."

Matney nodded. "It's strange that the whole time the car has been sitting there, no lights have come on in either the house or the vehicle."

"Did you pick up on the lack of radio chatter in the background while I was talking with Aubrey?"

"I thought it was her headphones blocking it out."

"Ha! As if Oak Grove can afford that quality of equipment."

"Every instinct is screaming at me that this is all wrong."

Jake agreed. It had every sign of being a setup. But who was the target? He couldn't imagine anyone going to these lengths to trap him.

"I sure would like to get in there," Matney said again.

Chapter 23

And there it was. The first red flag. Did the FBI agent expect Jake to volunteer to break into Thomason's house?

Matney pulled out his wallet and ruffled through a few receipts. "Do you have a paper clip on you?"

Jake did. One that had been straightened and sewn into the hem of his pants. Old habits die hard. He wouldn't reveal it to Matney. "Maybe? Seems like some of the paperwork I got at City Hall a couple of days ago had one. Why?"

"I took a workshop in lock picking years ago. Thought I'd try my hand at it."

"You realize the man who lives there is a cop and has a gun."

"You realize I am law enforcement and I have several guns."

Jake scrounged around in his jacket's pockets and retrieved the requested paperclip. "You could try knocking on the front door first."

"And lose the element of surprise?"

He had a point. "Do you want me to come with you?"

The agent reached for his door handle. "I can't ask a civilian to get involved."

"I already am." Jake opened his door as the patrol car moved away, as silently as it had arrived.

"Now is as good of a time as any," Matney said, opening his door. "I'll go in first. Your job is to assure the cop and his wife I'm legit. You want a gun?"

"I'm an ex-felon, Agent. I'm not giving anyone an excuse to shoot at me."

"You don't fit the profile and I forgot. Follow me."

Ages ago, Jake had spent a few days with Thomason in the middle of a snowstorm. His back yard looked much the same as it did then, minus the snow. One tree with its leaves gone, four bushes, and a small patio. Standard Oak Grove setup.

An extension of the roof protected the back door. The outside light to the right was either turned off or blown out. Matney bumped his foot against the step leading to the cement landing pad, but caught himself.

He fumbled inserting the paperclip in the lock and dropped it. It pinged on the concrete. He pulled a small flashlight from his pocket and shone it on the ground. The paperclip glittered in the light and Matney picked it up. He handed the flashlight to Jake and tipped his head towards the door.

Jake could have had the door unlocked by now, but he had a game to play. So, he shone the light on the lock and let the agent have his moment of glory.

He heard the first tumbler drop and held his breath. If he remembered correctly, and if Thomason hadn't changed the lock, there were five more to go.

Matney's hand jerked, and he swore under his breath. Jake wasn't surprised. The agent had lost his concentration and would need to start over. He held the light in place and pretended he was stone. What Jake wanted to do was push the FBI man aside and do the job himself.

Then the agent squared his shoulders and settled into place. The first pin drop came quicker this time, the second one even faster. Matney had got the hang of it, and soon, six tumblers had fallen. Still, Jake took a deep breath when the agent reached for the doorknob.

It opened easily. No one yelled, no lights were turned on, no shots were fired. Jake didn't know what he'd expected, but it wasn't this eerie quiet.

"Kitchen first," Jake whispered. "Small dining room, then the living room. Hall off the dining area with 3 bedrooms, one bath. There's a coat closet by the front door."

Matney nodded and didn't ask questions, but Jake realized those would come later. The agent stuck the paperclip into his pocket and retrieved his weapon from its holster. He crouched, pushed the door open the rest of the way, and entered the kitchen, his hands holding his gun outstretched, sweeping from side to side.

There was no response. Not a scream or a whimper. Jake feared the worst. He followed Matney inside.

The agent repeated his actions in the dining and living rooms, but Jake stayed in the kitchen. He returned to where Jake waited in the hallway and shook his head.

The search of the bedrooms was anticlimactic. The Thomasons weren't there.

Jake and Matney sat in the car across the street, watching nothing happen. "Where did they go?" Matney asked.

To Jake, it had all the signs of an intentional last-minute disappearance, with the refrigerator still filled with food and Sarah's car in the garage. No sign of a struggle or clothes being gone. Only one piece puzzled him—Sarah's purse was on the dresser in the bedroom.

"Do you have the equipment to triangulate on their phones' last known location?" Jake asked.

"Agent Jackson is working on it."

"What does Chief Santos have to say?"

"He thinks we're overreacting based on information from an unreliable source."

"Me."

"You. His theory is that Thomason and his wife took off to get away for a night and relieve the stress he's been under. He expects he'll either show up for his shift or call in."

Jake yawned and didn't bother covering his mouth. He'd had a short, unplanned nap while Matney had made phone calls from the bumper of the car. "I'd buy into it if his patrol vehicle hadn't fallen off the GPS and Sarah's purse didn't get left behind."

"I agree. But we're keeping our investigation on a

need-to-know basis, based on Santos' request. And we decided he doesn't qualify. That may change when our DHS incident commander gets here."

"Did you see if Sarah's phone was in her purse? Or her meds?" Did Sarah have more than one purse? Jake had never paid attention. Most women did.

"Her phone wasn't there." Matney rubbed a hand over the top of his head. "I'm not sure about a pill case."

"That could be bad news. She has occasional panic attacks and if she doesn't have her medication, she'll melt down. Has anyone told Harmony?"

"Jackson says she's still sleeping."

"What time is it?"

"About five. Not quite sunrise."

Jake stretched. "I'm going to need lots of coffee to make it through the day."

"DHS requested more people from various agencies to join the task force, including two female deputies. The female part was specified, which isn't normal. The point is, you'll be able to take some downtime and take a nap. Me, too."

"Any update on Houck?"

"The FASS agent?"

Jake nodded.

Matney fiddled with his watch. "He's holding his own. That's all they'll tell us. We've made no progress in identifying who was responsible, but we *will* find him."

A black sedan pulled in front of Thomason's house and parked. "There's my relief. I'll be right back."

Jake figured this could take a while. He leaned back in his seat and closed his eyes.

He opened them again when Matney slid into the driver's seat. "Sorry that took so long. You ready to roll?"

"Can you drop me off at my place? I need to shower and change clothes. Besides, hanging around you LEO types isn't my idea of a fun day."

"No can do. The incident commander has requested to meet with you."

"People keep using that phrase, and no one ever uses his name. Who is this guy?"

"He is a she. She's practically a legend. Special Assistant Vanessa Salters."

The last meeting Jake had with Salters was after Harmony and Eli's wedding, when the then-ATF Special Agent had warned him to stay out of Harmony's life. Jake didn't anticipate this meeting going any better.

In front of the Formby house, Matney double-parked alongside a full-size black van arrayed with an assortment of antennas. "Mobile command center," Matney explained. "Self-contained with a variety of electronic equipment. I assume that's how Mrs. Salters traveled. That way, she could be in touch when she was on the road."

Mrs. Salters? At least Jake knew how to address her.

"I'm supposed to take you inside to the command center, then report to the officer of the day. After that, who knows?" Matney stuck out his hand. "In case I don't see you again, I wanted to say that I don't believe half of what I was told about you. You take care of yourself."

What was that supposed to mean? Jake shook the agent's hand, anyway. "Good luck."

They walked side by side to the open front door and Matney waved for Jake to go in first. There were three desks crammed into the front room with various pieces of equipment piled on them. Only one of them was occupied.

The older man looked up as they entered. Jake assumed he was FBI, based on the black suit. Definitely not a marshal, probably not FASS, and who knew about the CIA?

Matney flashed his ID. "Mrs. Salters is expecting us. Well, him anyway."

"She's upstairs, in the room at the end of the hallway. She may be on a conference call, but we've put a couple of chairs outside."

"Thanks."

They headed upstairs, Jake a step behind, pretending he wasn't familiar with the layout. He wasn't looking forward to the upcoming confrontation.

The door at the end was halfway closed. Matney knocked softly.

"If that's Jake Hennessey, come in."

"Good luck," Matney whispered.

Jake would need the luck. He grabbed the door handle and pushed. Behind the desk, the lady's back was turned to him. She shuffled papers, and that gave him a chance to adjust his bearings and prepare for battle.

He sat in the empty chair on his side of the room and crossed his legs. Casual but in charge.

Her chair squeaked as she swiveled to face him. Her eyes raked Jake from head to foot, and he sat quietly until her inspection was complete. He used the moment to assess her.

Vanessa Salters hadn't changed—much. There was gray mixed in with her blond hair, and small wrinkles on her face that added character. She was as slim as he remembered, although she moved with more deliberation.

"You haven't whisked Harmony away," she said.

"I offered. She turned me down. And congratulations on your marriage," Jake said. "I wasn't aware of it, or I would have sent a present."

She laughed. "I can see me trying to explain that to my husband. Oh, he's a jewel thief who helped me protect a witness and solve an attempted murder."

"I've never been found guilty of any theft," Jake parried.

"I've kept track of you. Does Las Vegas ring a bell?"

"I was in Chicago."

"And Houston?"

Jake spread his arms. "I was here, attending a city council meeting. The agencies involved had to retract their charges." He doubted she was aware of Little Rock or a dozen other towns he'd "visited."

She put her forearms on the desk and leaned forward. "You swore you'd stay away from Harmony. You've broken our agreement."

"She came looking for me."

"You're too slick. I don't trust you."

It was Jake's turn to lean forward. "You shouldn't. In fact, you shouldn't trust anyone until this mess is straightened out. Don't believe half of what you have in the files, either. It's speculation and I can't find a morsel of truth."

"Except for Harmony?"

"You haven't talked to her yet?"

"No, we had a phone chat before I left DC, but I'm told she's sleeping."

"When was the last time you saw her in person?"

"Shortly after the accident. Which may not have been an accident at all. But we kept in contact. What difference does it make?"

"When you finally see her, be sure to look her in the eyes when she talks—if she lets you. She's hiding something, and lying with every breath."

Vanessa shook her head. "This feels like an elaborate practical joke. Harmony lying? And the ex-con who is more concerned about one of the town's cops disappearing than the Chief of Police?"

"I hoped you had information that would help everything make sense."

"If you expect me to pull out a magic wand, it won't happen. What I can do is include resources from a variety of agencies. That's in place. We'll get to the bottom of this."

That sounded like a dismissal to Jake. He stood and extended his hand. "Under these circumstances, I won't say it's nice to see you again, but I hope we can get along long enough to ensure Harmony's safety."

"You're the one needing protection from what I can tell." Salters cocked her head as she grasped his hand.

He smiled wryly. "It's a role I'm not used to."

Jake wrangled his car between the government vehicles parked on either side of the street. He needed a shower, a nap, and fresh clothes—not necessarily in that order—which meant a trip to his apartment. When a car pulled out behind him, he didn't give it a second thought. He assumed the FBI's file on him contained his address, and was too tired to pretend otherwise. He'd save his energy for a game of hide-n-go-seek later, if it was needed.

Chapter 24

"I'd expect this from a reckless teen, but not from you, Hennessey," Trina, the nurse at the clinic, scolded. She shoved a stray lock of her black hair behind her ear. "I'll have to get Doc Gabe to order a new batch of x-rays and start over!"

"It's not my blood," Jake protested. He was glad to see her back. "I just don't want people to have to look at it. Or be reminded of where it came from."

She stared at him. "Shit, you were at the accident last night. I heard it was bad."

Jake nodded. "There wasn't much I could do to help. Remind me to take a first-aid class the next time it's offered."

"I'll make a note. Sit tight and I'll be right back."

"Are you in trouble?" Trina asked when she returned with the supplies she needed. "It appears you have a shadow hanging out in the waiting room."

"Dressed in black?" he asked. "FBI. I've become a person of some importance to them."

"Do you need rescued?"

"No. They are protecting me. At least, I'm letting them think they are."

"Right." She was cutting the old cast with the saw and stopped where Thomason had dug out the tracker. "What happened here?"

"The tech who filled in for you didn't meet the clinic's normal standards."

"Rumors say he spent way too much time hanging around with a cop. We won't have him back again." She took the last of the cast pieces off and started washing his arm.

"You know which cop it was?"

"Morrison, I think."

It seemed too convenient. "I've never dealt with him."

She glanced up from her work. "Aren't you the lucky one. He's a local boy and should know better, but it is what it is."

While Trina applied the new cast, Jake stared at the ceiling and reevaluated his plans. With Thomason out of the picture, who could he go to for information? He didn't want to involve Aubrey, the 9-1-1 operator, and couldn't visit Krunk with the FBI in tow. What records would Salters be able to access on the sly?

Once he'd been released, he walked out to his car and waited for the FBI man to follow. Agent Matney wasn't trying to hide—just the opposite—so Jake didn't feel bad about approaching him.

"Let me guess," Jake said. "Your assignment is to

discourage anyone from attacking me while letting me go about my business."

"At least until the two additional deputy marshals Mrs. Salters requested arrive."

"How did you get stuck with me?"

"I volunteered."

"Sorry to disappoint you. You watched me sleep for four hours. Are you able to feed me information? Like, has there been any word on Thomason?"

"The detective? No. And Chief Santos isn't cooperating."

Jake leaned against the agent's car and stared at his shoes. "How about Houck?" He might not wear the agent's blood anymore, but he still carried a level of guilt for Houck getting hurt.

"No word. That means he hasn't died, right?"

"Right."

Matney joined Jake in leaning against the car. "You can call me Sam, by the way. There'll be lots of us that come and go, but I'll be sticking around."

"How much trouble are you willing to get into, Sam?"

The agent's lips twitched. "Honestly? I'm considered boring, doing everything by the book. I deal mostly with financial crimes, and I'm good at what I do. That's why I was brought in—someone figured I'd be able to handle Mrs. Duprie. But if I want to get better, I have to take chances. I read your record. If anyone can destroy my reputation, it's you. What do you have in mind?"

They took Jake's car and headed towards Thomason's

house. "Is someone watching the house? Front and back?" Jake asked.

"Electronic, only in front. We don't have the personnel or the equipment. We asked Chief Santos to provide a patrol, but my reports say they've only sent a cruiser down the street twice in the last five hours."

"That makes it too easy."

"What are you planning, Hennessey?"

Jake grinned. "Step one in loosening up. Call me Jake. It'll drive your co-workers nuts."

"What's step two?"

"We're going to break into Thomason's house again. I figure we can spot more clues in the daylight."

"What's the deal between you and Thomason? Why do you care so much?"

Jake waited patiently at a stop sign while a school bus drove by on the cross street. "He busted me my first and only time. The initial charge was bogus, but I earned my prison term by beating the crap out of him and two patrolmen. When I was released a couple of years later, he let me stay with him during a blizzard. I've had his back a time or two, he's always been straight with me, and I figure I still owe him."

"No one would believe me if I told them that story."

"Nope. And he'd bust me again if he caught me breaking the law. So, just say I'm trying to be a good citizen." Jake proceeded through the intersection and turned down an alley.

"They won't accept that one either."

"Do you still have that paperclip on you?"

"No. I changed clothes while you met with Mrs. Salters."

That wouldn't be a problem for Jake. He had several innocent-looking metal scraps in his glovebox and under his seat he could use. "We should double check you remembered to lock the door last night."

Sam nodded his head and then broke into a grin. "That's a great idea."

The convenience store a block away from Thomason's house provided the cover Jake wanted. He didn't explain his plan to the agent—it was a test, of sorts.

"Hey, Gracie," he called as he entered, the electric bell dinging. Sam was right behind him.

"Hey yourself," the white-haired lady hollered back. "What's up?"

"Not much." Jake studied the choice of candy bars. Sam moved into the next aisle, where the medicines were displayed.

They weren't the only customers. The lottery was up to a record-setting prize and a long line of people waited for their chance at a better life. Jake avoided the crowd and headed towards the back hallway. Sam followed.

They left out the rear entrance, passed the dumpsters, and down the alley.

"That was slick," Sam said.

"But easy to figure out. You still have your phone on you, correct? And a smart watch?"

"Gotcha. I've never gone undercover. Do you want me to ditch them?"

"No. I'm just pointing it out for future reference. Besides, we don't want to alarm anyone with another LEO going off-grid."

They wove their way around garbage cans and

cardboard boxes filled with debris. "Normally there isn't this much trash back here," Jake explained. "Pick up day is tomorrow."

"Which means lots of potential evidence for easy pickings. Early in my career, I spent a few days working with gloves and a mask as I analyzed documents pulled from a dumpster."

"I once helped a customer dig through the bar's garbage looking for his dentures." That had been a disgusting mess, but Jake had known the old man didn't have the money to replace them. "He found them at home the next day."

They reached the spot behind Thomason's house and Jake stopped behind an evergreen bush to look for anything out of place. Everything appeared normal. There should have been cops everywhere, looking for clues to Thomason's disappearance. Instead, there was one bean-counter FBI agent and a beat-up old jewel thief.

He strolled towards the back door like he owned the place. He reached for the handle to check if it was unlocked. By the time Sam caught up to him, it was.

"After you," he said, opening the door a crack and stepping aside. "You're the one with a gun."

Jake studied the agent's form as he entered the house. Sam might be a desk jockey, but he'd kept up on his training. Perfect form, gun held correctly, his movements clean and precise. It made Jake wonder how much of what he'd been told about the agent's background was true. By the time the agent finished checking out the house, Jake sat at the dining room table, going through Sarah's purse.

It was more of a briefcase, with a variety of tools Sarah used when she showed homes. Pens of various colors, three notepads, two flashlights, business cards, an assortment of paperwork, and a tablet for clients who had a hard time reading their phones. What wasn't there was what Jake jokingly referred to as her "inside purse," a smaller organizer that held her money, credit card, and ID. It was good that it wasn't there. What was bad was that her pill case was. At least, until he stuffed it in his pocket.

"Sam," he called. "Check the bedroom. See if you can spot Sarah's meds."

Jake went to check the kitchen cupboards. He had no idea where Sarah might store them.

"Are these what you're looking for?" Sam asked, holding out two separate medicine bottles.

Jake took them and examined the labels, but didn't recognize the names. "Can you look them up?"

"No need. My mother had more prescriptions than I thought necessary before her death." Sam held up one container. "This one is blood pressure." He held up the other one. "This is a basic anti-anxiety pill. You said she has panic attacks? I'm guessing that's what these are for."

That wasn't good.

"Not to state the obvious, but we need to find them." Jake closed the kitchen cabinet he'd been searching. He didn't want to leave the house a mess. "Were you folks able to triangulate on their phones' last known location?"

"Hold on." Sam fiddled with his phone, and Jake walked through the living room. No obvious signs of a struggle, but he wasn't an expert. Everything seemed to be in place, down to the decorative crystal balls on the coffee table in the front room.

"Both phones last connected from here," Sam said. "So, I'm confused. If they left their phones behind, where are they? If they had been snatched and had their phones, we should have picked up the signal at their new location. But if they remembered to take out the sim cards, why did they leave Mrs. Thomason's pills behind?"

"Has anyone checked for activity on their bank accounts?" Jake stared out the window towards the backyard. Nothing, besides a robin looking for bugs, moved.

"We need a warrant for that. Since Chief Santos hasn't been helpful, we've held off. It'll be up to Mrs. Salters to make that decision." Sam shrugged. "Here I thought I was getting away from the financial transaction line of work."

"With your background, you'll know exactly what to say to Mrs. Salters to get her to approve your request. Bonus points for you," Jake said.

Jake drove up next to Sam's car at the clinic. "It's been fun," he said, "but here's where we split up."

"You're not going back to Mrs. Duprie's?"

"It's better if I don't. Give Harmony and Vanessa time to catch up."

"Vanessa?"

Jake grinned. "Mrs. Salters. This isn't our first time working together to protect Harmony."

Sam's jaw dropped. "That's not in the file."

"It was unofficial. She didn't like me any better back then than she does now. But she's fair and won't let that influence her opinion of you."

"It doesn't matter. My job is to protect you."

Jake suddenly understood why Harmony hated bodyguards. "Here's the problem. I need to go a few places you can't, talk to people who will shun me if you're around. No matter how you dress down, you'll be identified as a Fed."

"You'll be careful?"

There were bars in and around Oak Grove where Jake was welcome, even if he was technically the competition. He and the owners clued each other in to information about alcohol board sting operations, undercover drug busts and the like. One of these, The Black Horse, was where Jake headed. It was out of city limits, and risky, because the motel the Feds were staying in was on the other side of the interstate exit. But it was his best bet for gossip.

"Rudy!" he called as he walked in. Heads swiveled to see who'd interrupted their quiet conversations. The small business wouldn't get noisy until more customers arrived and loosened up after a couple of drinks.

"Hennessey!" Rudy called back. "I figured you'd be in Cleveland since your place is out of business. Whatcha drinking?"

"Whiskey. Make it a double." He took a seat on a patched bar stool. "I've been taking care of personal issues in my downtime."

The generous pour came from one of the middle-shelf bottles. When Rudy set it in front of him, Jake raised it in an appreciative salute.

"You running a tab tonight?" Rudy asked.

"I wish. But there's an influx of law enforcement types in town, and I'm playing it safe."

"Yep. I heard one of them got hit by a car."

The balding man a few stools down joined the conversation. "I heard that's why they brought in the 'copter. It must have been bad."

"Any of us would go by ambulance." Jake recognized the new speaker. Coulson considered himself a political activist, but most of the time he was just a pain in the neck. He came over and sat beside Jake. "They didn't airlift you to Pittsburgh to be treated."

Jake sipped his whiskey and found it unexpectedly smooth and rich. He arched his eyebrows and nodded to Rudy to express his appreciation. "Thank God I didn't need to go," he said. "I would have been miserable laying in a hard hospital bed in a too-cold room with a grumpy old nurse."

The laughter that followed assured Jake that he was one of them and they wouldn't keep secrets from him.

Jake slept in his own bed, knowing that no one would get past Salters and her team.

Chapter 23

Jake stood in the kitchen of Harmony's house, waiting for the water to finish cycling through the coffee pad when Salters burst in.

"Hennessey! How the hell did you get in?" she asked, lowering her revolver.

"Good morning to you, too." Jake had heard her coming down the stairs, but wanted to see her reaction. He jerked his head towards the back door. "I have the code. I take care of the place when it isn't being used."

"I didn't come across that information in the files."

"Probably not." Jake picked up the mug and sniffed the brew. He wished he'd had the chance to add a shot of rum, but that would wait. "I did it as a personal favor for Eli."

"And it let you keep tabs on Harmony."

"Actually, no. She was in good hands. Eli treated her like she deserved to be treated." Something Jake couldn't do.

Salters pushed past him and grabbed a cup off the mug tree. "What are your motives, Hennessey?"

He sipped the steaming coffee, then took a deep swallow, reveling in the warmth of the liquid running down the back of his throat. "I thought I wanted her to be happy. Spend time with friends, work a job she loves, have time to read. Now I'm hoping she can find some peace."

Salters put her cup on the coffeemaker and waited for it to do its magic. "Yesterday, I saw what you meant about her lying. I didn't realize it was that bad."

"She's not as good at hiding it as she thinks she is." Jake clutched his cup with both hands. "But it's your turn to tell the truth. Was the threat against Angel ever as bad as Houck and FASS made it out to be?"

She removed her cup from the maker and stirred in a spoonful of sugar. "We're having a second translator go through the document. I'm told two passages can be interpreted differently depending upon which dialect the writer used."

Salters blew across the top of her coffee. "I'm reviewing the paperwork about the incident that killed Eli and injured Harmony. I read many of them before the official report was issued and don't remember anything that would point to it being more than an accident."

"Angel is going to want to see those files."

"I won't make that call on my own. It'll be up to her therapist."

Jake wasn't sure the decision should be taken away from Harmony, but it wasn't under his control, and not a battle he could win.

They stood in the kitchen drinking their brew, not talking, not looking at each other. It was Salters' move.

Jake was an expert at the waiting game. He'd drained his cup and was washing it when she broke.

"What are you doing here, Hennessey?"

"We covered that." He flashed his best smile.

Salters glared at him. "That's not what I mean. You ditched Agent Matney last night and wander in here this morning like you own the place. What are you up to?"

"The same as you. Gathering information. We need each other."

"What can you do that my team can't?"

"You know better than that, Vanessa." He used her first name as a reminder that he didn't work for or answer to her. "Your folks aren't familiar with Oak Grove and the residents don't know you. You think they'll share their deepest secrets with your team?"

"So, we trade tit-for-tat?"

"And keep score? No." He put his cup back on the mug tree. "There will be things you can't tell me. I understand that. But stop considering me an enemy."

"You've already corrupted Agent Matney."

"Corrupted? No. Sam will be a better agent when I get done with him."

"Then why didn't you take him along last night?"

"I was hunting for info on Thomason."

Salters cocked her head. "The detective?"

Jake nodded. "And his wife. They are both Harmony's friends. But the rumor mill isn't even aware they're missing. How is that possible unless Chief Santos has it locked down while pretending it's no big deal?"

"What's your theory?"

"I have two. I can't make either of them connect."

A muffled, rhythmic thunking on the carpeted living room floor alerted them to Harmony's approach. "Does she know?" Jake whispered.

Salters shook her head. "You have your first cup of coffee yet, Harmony?" she asked loudly.

"No, I was just coming to get one." Harmony stopped in the doorway. "You two haven't killed each other?"

Jake started the process of making Harmony a cup of coffee. "We are discussing the ground rules on maintaining a working relationship. No death threats involved. Not yet, anyway."

"You didn't come back last night, Jake."

She'd noticed. "I went home. I wanted to give you and Vanessa the chance to talk without worrying about me eavesdropping."

"And you got to sleep in a bed instead of a chair."

Jake grinned. "No comment."

He added cream and sugar to the cup and handed the coffee to Harmony. "Do you have any plans for the day?"

"I'd suggest going for a ride somewhere, but the last time we tried, it didn't work out so well."

"I'd like you to look at a few files, Harmony," Salters said.

"And I have a meeting with Rochelle, my lead contractor," Jake said. "We're debating the placement of the door when we rebuild the front of the bar. You two have fun, and I'll check in later."

"What are you planning, Hennessey?" Salters asked as she trailed him out the door.

"I really should get with Rochelle," Jake answered. "Is Sam going to be shadowing me again today?"

"Why? Do you have more houses to break into?"

So, Sam had reported on their adventure. Jake stopped at the bottom of the stairs. "As a broker, Sarah has access to most of the homes that are for sale in the area. She knows which ones are occupied and which ones aren't. What if she and Thomason are using one as a safe house?"

"How many houses are we talking about?"

"Twenty-five or so. But the listings are online so it won't be hard to find them."

"What are you waiting for?"

Sam stared at the list on his phone. "How do you want to approach this? Grid pattern?"

"I want to narrow it down. First, places with a garage where a cop car could hide. Second, places near a convenience store where they could get food."

"Would they be recognized if they go out?"

"It's a possibility."

"Anything else?"

Jake stroked the steering wheel. "The other thing I'd like to figure out is which neighborhoods have a 'Nosy Nessie.' Thomason would avoid a house there."

"You don't have that info?"

Jake chuckled. "There are 'good' people in this town that avoid the likes of me." He made air quotes around the word *good*.

"I don't know if it meets your criteria," Sam said, studying his phone's screen, "But there's a house three blocks from here. Seems like an easy place to start."

The red SUV in the driveway, the kids' toys on the porch, and the harvest-colors flag flying made it clear the two-story house on Buckeye Street was occupied. Jake didn't slow down.

"That's a nice place," Sam said.

"But overpriced for the market. It would sell for twice as much in Pittsburgh. What's next on the list?"

The fourth house Jake picked held promise. Quiet neighborhood, garage, fenced yard for privacy. But it needed a new roof, so it had been for sale for months.

Jake parked across the street, half a block away, and he and Sam observed the house.

"Curtains are closed," Sam said. "That seems odd. What are we waiting for?"

"I still wonder if the cops are involved, or Thomason disappeared on his own." Jake unfastened his seat belt. "I don't want to walk in on a hostage situation without preparation."

Sam copied his action. "Yeah, it seemed suspicious when the cop sat in front of his house the other night."

"Do you have access to the secure band yet?"

"The chief has been stonewalling us. We don't want the cops listening to ours, so we set up a separate one."

Jake glanced in his rear-view mirror. "Oh, look. We have company."

A police car pulled in behind them and flashed its strobe lights.

"Let me handle this," Sam said, reaching into his jacket pocket and pulling out his badge. He laid it on the dashboard.

Jake recognized the cop before she reached the car and rolled down his window. "How can I help you, Officer Bellevue?"

She looked startled. "Mr. Hennessey. I wasn't expecting you. We got a report about a suspicious car in the neighborhood, and they assigned it to me."

"I pulled over to make a phone call. I see they're letting you work on your own. That's good. You deserve it."

One corner of her mouth lifted. "Nuisance calls, that's all, but it's a start. Gets me away from the paperwork and the stress. Everyone's on edge with the Feds in town."

Sam coughed.

"Officer Bellevue," Jake said, grinning. "Meet Agent Sam Matney, FBI. He got the short end of the stick and was assigned as my shadow. I'm sorry, Officer, but I don't know your first name."

Sam leaned past Jake and put his hand out the window. "Pleased to meet you, Officer Bellevue. Aren't you one of the officers that responded to the scene of the shooting a few days ago?"

"Yes, sir," Bellevue answered.

"Good job on that report. Thorough and well-written."

Bellevue blushed. "Thank you, sir."

"Are you due for a break, Officer?" Sam asked. "I want to get your thoughts on how that incident relates to what happened the other night. Can I buy you a coffee?"

Her eyes widened. "I'd like that. Let me call it in."

"What are you up to?" Jake asked when Bellevue walked back to her car.

"I want to pump her for information about the inter-office politics at the station. She probably hasn't picked a side yet."

"She may not talk around me."

"I'm sure you can create an excuse to give us privacy. Maybe you need to follow up on that phone call you pulled over for."

Who's manipulating who? At least Jake hadn't revealed any of his deepest secrets to Sam yet.

Jake put his coffee into the cup holder when Sam opened the car door. He'd spent his down time checking in with Danny in Cleveland, where everything was running smoothly. "Any luck?"

"Officer Wanda Bellevue is a bright young woman," Sam said. "But this is her first professional job, and she hasn't figured out the whole office politics concept. There's a lot of information that is being kept from her. She believes Thomason is out on medical leave."

"Good cover story, but it doesn't give us a clue to how and why he disappeared."

"Which puts us right back to chasing down empty houses."

"Except I was thinking about it while I was sitting out here. All those houses are for sale, and other realtors can show them. They aren't as safe as they seem."

"I hear a but coming on."

"How about a house that is empty but not for sale?"

"You have one in mind?"

"Mine."

"It makes sense," Jake explained as they headed towards a different neighborhood. "I took it off the market, so there'll be no showings. The house is staged and there's enough furniture to make it livable. All the utilities are turned on, too."

"Wouldn't it be risky to go back? Or are you thinking lightning doesn't strike twice?" Sam asked.

"Precisely."

"And if they aren't there?"

"Oak Grove is a dying town. There are lots of empty houses. Thomason could have come across one suitable for a hideout."

Chapter 26

Jake parked a block away from the remodeled home. The trees had shed their leaves for the winter, but the other homes hid his house. He left the car running and just sat there.

"Is there a problem?" Sam asked.

"What if Thomason and Sarah are there?" Jake asked. "Am I putting them in danger if I find them? I don't even know what they are hiding from. If they are hiding."

"You won't be alone in protecting them. There are half a dozen agencies involved."

"That didn't protect Houck."

Sam's shoulders sagged. "No, it didn't."

"How is he doing? I haven't heard."

"He's hanging on. That's all we've been told. But I thought you don't like him."

"Is that what the report says? Because it's right. He was full of himself, and didn't have the foggiest idea of how to protect Harmony. Still, I feel guilty he was run over. I'm convinced I was the intended target."

"What makes you say that?"

"Have you watched the video, Sam?"

"Are there any other videos from that night?" the agent asked after watching the replay on his cell phone for the third time.

"There should be. Houck had monitoring equipment in the attic. But this is the only one I've seen."

"I can see your point. From this video, it's clear who is who. But out on the street—not so much. I want to view it from a different angle and on a bigger screen."

"Was that part of the investigation handled by your people, or Oak Grove's finest?" Jake asked. "Who may or may not have reasons to hide evidence?"

"Which is your priority? To go to headquarters and review what we have, or check if the Thomasons are at your house?"

He was so close. And Jake really wanted to get Sarah's meds to her. "We'll drive down the alley," he said. "See if anything looks out of place. Then we can head back."

The oversized dining room of the Formby house had been converted to a meeting room and a large monitor had been mounted on one wall. It displayed three separate videos of Houck being run over. Seeing it repeatedly didn't help the twisting in Jake's gut.

He wasn't alone. There were six others, including Sam and Salters.

"We've got Hennessey sitting right here," Sam

said, "but in the video taken from the attic, you could convince me that's him walking across the street. The way Houck was holding the cake container, it resembled a cast."

"What's the motive?" Salters asked. "Nothing I've seen in any of the police reports touches on it. Hennessey?"

"All I have are theories." Jake filled his glass with ice water from a pitcher on the folding table. "At first, I thought Houck was involved because he warned me away from Harmony before the funeral. I wasn't sure if he was trying to scare me out of town or setting me up to do something illegal."

"I have several follow-up questions, but let's start with the easiest," Salters said. "You implied you no longer believe Houck was involved. Why not?"

"He doesn't have the local connections needed. Most of the attacks happened at random times, when there'd be no lead time to set them up."

"Wasn't Special Agent Houck a target of one attack?" asked an agent Jake hadn't met yet. Jake pegged him as a hard case that would never give Jake a fair shot and labeled him as Agent HC.

"Yes. That's why I took him off my list of suspects."

"He suggested you saved his life."

Jake shook his head. "I'm not convinced the shot wasn't aimed at me."

"So, if Houck isn't responsible, who is?" The agent drummed his fingers on the tabletop.

"The only thing I can come up with is someone connected to the local police."

"I'm sure you have enemies, Mr. Hennessey, or is it easier to blame the attacks on law enforcement?" Agent HC smirked.

"Let's keep this professional," Salters snapped.

Jake shrugged. "It's a fair question. Of course, I have enemies. But none with the time, energy, or resources to pull off these attacks. They're more likely to run a happy hour promo to steal my customers, not kill me."

"Does that happen often?" Sam asked.

"Off and on. It's almost a game."

"Where does Detective Thomason fit?" HC asked.

Salters pushed her chair away from the table. "That's up to us to figure out. Has anyone interviewed the officer who ran patrol the night of the incident? Maybe they went through the detective's neighborhood, too."

Nobody spoke.

"What? Didn't anyone else watch the whole tape?" She chose the control to rewind the video. The display started where Jake and Houck walked out the front door of Harmony's house. As they stood and talked, a patrol car could be seen in the background. "Somebody get that officer's name and bring them here for an interview," she ordered.

That put an end to the meeting. The room emptied, except for Jake and Sam. Jake stared at the screen, where the frame with the police car remained.

"You seeing something we missed?" Sam asked.

"No." Jake shook his head. "It's a cop car like every other cop car in Oak Grove. The lighting isn't right to see the driver or the identifying number. It could be anyone."

"Staring at it won't change that. Let's get lunch. There are sandwiches in the kitchen."

There weren't any security cameras on the back side of the Formby house. Not that Jake could spot from the kitchen windows. He supposed they weren't needed, although much of the equipment inside the house would sell for big bucks on the black market. Even the tablet left lying on the kitchen counter could bring in enough of a payout to buy a bottle of aged whiskey.

He amused himself by plotting a path from the door, past the cluster of cars parked in the yard, through the gate, and down the alley. He could stash the tablet under the neighbor's garbage can and retrieve it later. Two minutes out and back in, and no one would know he'd been gone.

"What are you thinking about, Hennessey?" Salters said from behind him.

He didn't turn. "That you need more security. Anyone can walk in here."

"And do what?"

"The coffee maker will bring a good fifty, seventy-five bucks. Shoot, the coffee pods will rake in an easy twenty-five. The tablet is a guaranteed several hundred. All of those are grab-n-go."

"I'll have it taken care of. I guess I got spoiled working in secure government buildings. But the fact you know these things doesn't increase my confidence in you."

Jake turned to face her. "The fact that you had my apartment searched doesn't make me trust you, either."

"Fair. At least we understand each other."

"We do."

Salters leaned against the counter. "I came to share information with you."

"Oh?"

"I heard from Chief Santos. He claims there was no unit patrolling this street at the time of the attack on Houck."

Jake blinked rapidly. "Is he stupid?"

"Or badly misguided by someone on his staff. I didn't reveal we had evidence to the contrary. Normally, I'd suggest infiltrating the force, but there's no time for it. There is an additional possibility."

"Which is?"

"That it was Detective Thomason, driving his patrol car with the GPS disabled. And what if he was working with whoever was in the car that hit Agent Houck?"

Jake felt he'd been kicked in the gut. "No. Not Thomason."

"I feel the same way, but we can't disregard any possibilities."

That made finding Thomason even more important. If word leaked to the local cops that he was a person of interest, there'd be no telling how he'd be treated. Jake knew all about that.

It meant he had to ditch Sam. And the rest of the Feds.

Jake knew old houses—the good, the bad, and every

feature he could take advantage of. In the case of the Formby house, the basement.

When they built the house, it only had outside access to the cellar. In the 1920s, a stairwell had been added in the kitchen with an outside door halfway down. It hadn't been used for years.

That didn't bother Jake. Spiders and cobwebs didn't scare him. He stashed his phone and his watch on the top shelf of a kitchen cupboard. He'd be going old-school.

The exterior cellar door opened on the west side of the house, under the bathroom window. Jake placed his bet on the speculation that no agent would push aside the dusty yellow curtains to look outside.

The door squeaked loudly as he pushed it open. He paused, waiting for someone to sound an alarm. None came.

Crouching, he dashed to the nearest car and crawled beside it towards the alley. Once behind the trunk, he prepared for the riskiest part. In full daylight, he'd have to cross between the cars and the garbage bin without cover. There was no skill involved in this step. It was pure luck, and that had been in short supply lately.

Jake chuckled at himself. He could have walked out any door. He wasn't under arrest and was free to leave. But then there'd be a record of it, and Sam or another agent would follow. This was as close as he would ever get to recreating his glory days.

He ignored the pain in his left knee as he rose. Arthritis, the doctor had said. Instinct guided his timing, and in a few seconds he was hidden by the garbage cans in the alley.

The rest should be easy, but he didn't trust that his car wasn't tagged. He'd left it a block away because parking spots by the Formby house were hard to find. He planned to drive it to the grocery store, leave it there, and walk the rest of the way to the house he had for sale. It wasn't a perfect plan, but was the best he could do.

The trip down the alley was uneventful, as was the drive to the grocery store. If anyone followed him, they deserved an award for being inconspicuous. He bought some snack crackers and exited out a different door. So far, so good.

But Jake had forgotten to account for the weather, and it started to sprinkle on his walk to the house. He didn't get any cover from the bare branches overhead, so he pulled his jacket closed and turned up his collar. It would be a miserable few blocks.

He walked up to the front door like he owned the place—which he did. If the Thomasons were inside, he wanted them to have a warning and lessen his chances of being greeted by a gun. The door and frame were new and opened without a creak, but he stomped heavily to knock away any leaves stuck to his shoes and to announce his presence.

The front room was empty, no surprise. Jake checked the kitchen, anticipating they'd have at least stocked the refrigerator with drinks, but it was as clean as the day it had been delivered. If his theory was wrong, he wasn't sure where to look next.

The alternative was the option he'd been ignoring. That the Thomasons were in trouble.

He continued his rounds through the house. Two bedrooms, two bathrooms, appearing to be untouched since the day of the shooting. There was one last place to look: the garage.

Which seemed darker than normal when he opened the connecting door. But it wasn't dark enough to hide the cop car sitting there, even if the small window in the back door had been covered.

Chapter 27

The car's heater was on full blast, and Jake was almost warm again when two black cars pulled in beside him in the grocery store parking lot, one on either side. So, he'd been right about one thing—they'd tagged his car.

Sam got out of the vehicle to his right and Jake leaned over and opened the door. The agent got in, closing the door.

"You're doing it wrong," Jake said. "You should have a car in front of me and one behind to keep me from getting away."

"You've been sitting here for an hour. I wasn't worried you'd leave. I was concerned something had happened."

"My car has been sitting here for an hour. That doesn't mean I was."

"I understand. Convincing Mrs. Salters that you aren't up to anything criminal was a challenge."

"Mrs. Salters hasn't forgiven me for existing."

Sam laughed. "She can be narrow-visioned."

"Says a man who has worked closely with her and

isn't your average FBI agent." Jake adjusted the heater, turning it down a notch.

"I'll confess. My specialty is cults. I told her I wouldn't fool you for long. What gave me away?" Sam asked.

"Little things. The big one was how easily you picked the lock at Thomason's house."

"I tried to make it seem hard."

"Good try."

"Says the guy who is supposedly a simple businessman and shouldn't know about picking locks. Is that where you went? Back to his house?"

"No, mine. They aren't there." Jake didn't mention the squad car in the garage.

"Salters took your idea of checking empty houses and ran with it. She has three agents out looking. It'll go faster that way."

"But the locals are more likely to get word."

Sam shrugged. "They're using the same cover story about a tip coming in reporting strange people hanging out where they don't belong. And they're verifying it has nothing to do with Mrs. Duprie."

It was vague and held a kernel of truth. "Are there any other updates?" Jake asked.

"You would think," the agent sighed, "that the combined forces of five U.S. agencies could prove or disprove the information that led to this situation. But, no, we're still waiting for the new translation of the source material. The gentleman doing it is hospitalized."

Jake clenched his jaw. "Another accident?"

"Nothing like that. Pneumonia, is my understanding."

Good news, Jake thought. *Since when is someone being sick good news?*

Sam's watch beeped, and Jake glanced at the display on the agent's wrist. But the readout was upside-down and tilted away from him, so he couldn't read it.

"Mrs. Salters is asking for an update," Sam said. "Mrs. Duprie noticed your absence and is concerned."

"Not a hint of manipulation there. But I don't want Harmony to worry, so I'll play it by the book. You taking the agency car, or do you want to ride with me?" Jake asked as he fastened his seatbelt.

"Sit tight." Sam hopped out of the car and went to talk to the two other agents. He was back in a minute, got in, closed the door, and strapped himself in. "We don't have to head straight back. Mrs. Salters is on a call with headquarters. She'll be tied up for a while."

Jake shifted the car into drive. "Anyplace in particular you want to go?"

"My great grandparents had a farm in this area. I don't know where, but I'd like to get out of town and away from the interstate and see the countryside. Any ideas?"

Harmony had introduced this road to him ages ago. Maintenance had been spotty since then, but it was passable, even the unpaved parts. There was one large farm on the dirt stretch that was still being worked. The fields would be bare this time of the year, but Jake figured it was the best local example of what he assumed Sam wanted to see.

Jake avoided as many mud puddles as possible as

they drove towards the farm. There were smaller homes along the way with their outbuildings in need of repair or of being torn down. Abandoned and dilapidated farm equipment dotted empty pastures. Even some houses still lived in were not being kept up. Money was tight everywhere.

Several places had four or five cars in the driveway or near the abandoned barns, but Jake didn't pay attention to them. It was typical for the houses to have more than one family sharing the home to make the rental cost more affordable. Another reflection of how the area had changed since its heyday.

Sam grunted as Jake tried to steer around a cluster of potholes.

"Sorry about that," Jake said. "I didn't realize how bad of a shape this road is in. The last few storms we've had must have done the damage."

"Either that or the wear and tear from the cars at the last house." Sam craned his neck to look behind them. "Must be close to a dozen."

"Someone having a party," Jake suggested.

"All newer models? It feels out -of -place."

"It's bugging you, isn't it?"

"Big time. Can we go back and check it out?"

Jake pulled onto a flat spot on the side of the road. "If it bothers you that much, we should. Are you prepared to destroy your clothes?"

Sam looked down at his black jacket, white shirt, black slacks, and black dress shoes and grimaced. "It won't be the first suit I've ruined in the line of duty, but I packed light for this trip."

He opened the car door and got out. "Coming?"

Jake's expertise didn't extend to sneaking through patches of trees and weeds. Neither did Sam's from the look of things, but he made a valiant effort, tromping through waist-high brush, and Jake followed. They crouched in the sparse cover of a clump of leafless bushes, close enough to see reflections from the windows of the house, but not inside.

"What now?" Jake asked.

Sam shoved a branch away from his face. "I'd like to get closer—check out a few license plates."

"There's only one window on this side of the house that doesn't have curtains. That helps." Jake studied the home with a practiced eye. "And it's in an odd spot, so I'm guessing it's in the stairwell."

"You know too much."

"I know old houses."

"What do you think is going on?"

Jake knew he was being led down a path he didn't want to travel. "That's your expertise, not mine. What's your guess?"

"Wrong time of day for a big game, and not enough noise for it to be a party. To me, it has the earmarks of an illegal operation. But not the counterfeit license plates, because there aren't any metallic noises or unpleasant odors."

"But those stickers that designate the year and month can be printed anywhere with the right paper. I threw a guy out of the bar last year when he tried to involve me in a scam of getting people to sell their real stickers and report them as stolen."

Sam cocked his head. "That bit of information might impact the investigation."

"Despite the bar's reputation, I run a clean business. Still, I deal with folks like that regularly. Them and people wanting donations to various causes, real or not. It'll lead to nothing but dead ends and wasted time trying to track down all of them. But the longer we stand here, the better chance for someone to see us."

"I guess this is all on me. You don't have your phone."

Had they found it?

"I'll be right back," Sam said, and took off.

Kneeling, Jake kept a watchful eye as the agent wove in and out of the eleven cars. There was no sign of movement from the building, not even someone outside smoking,

The faint hum of a car in the distance caught his attention, and he lay flat on the ground. The weeds between him and the road provided limited cover. Not enough to hide him from sharp eyes, but there wasn't anything else available. He hoped Sam found a better place.

He listened to the whine of the engine and waited for it to pass by. Except, from the sound, it joined the other cars at the house.

Jake propped himself on his elbows. The added height didn't give him a view of what was happening, so he pushed himself to his hands and knees. Through a cluster of dried grass, he made out two men exiting the vehicle with their backs to him. They wore heavy winter coats, hiding details of their appearance.

He ducked as the men turned and stretched. In those

few seconds, he'd assured himself that Sam was unseen. Jake hoped he'd gotten a better view of the new arrivals.

The next move was the agent's. All Jake could do was wait. He didn't like it.

For the second time, Jake sat in his car with the heat running on full blast. Half of the hot air was directed towards Sam. The agent remained silent, flipping through the pictures he'd taken and not sharing them with Jake. So much for working as partners.

"What are we waiting for?" he asked, changing the heater controls to defrost.

"Give me a minute." Another message popped up on the screen of Sam's phone, but Jake couldn't read it. "So far, the plates are coming up clean, but the transponders aren't working. We're only halfway through, so things could change."

"Which isn't illegal, because they aren't on the road," Jake pointed out. "It's a gray area."

"Yes. And nothing that any of the agencies in the task force have any jurisdiction over."

"Another dead end."

"Except for one thing." Sam handed his phone to Jake. "Tell me if you recognize the men in the picture."

It was a terrible photo, and the faces were blurred. But they seemed familiar, so Jake tapped on the screen to enlarge the display. It didn't help.

"You saw them. What do you think?" He moved the phone closer, as if that would correct the distortion.

"Neither look familiar."

Something about the man on the right bugged Jake. He crossed his eyes and focused on the picture as he uncrossed them. There was an old myth that it fooled the brain into correcting a blurred photo.

Once Jake had seen it, he couldn't convince himself of anything different. He handed the phone to Sam.

"What?" the agent asked.

"Thomason. That's Detective Thomason."

Sam studied the image. His watch pinged, and he glanced at it. "You're absolutely sure that's Thomason?"

"Let's say ninety percent. Why?"

"Two of those cars came back as having fake plates. One has plates reported stolen. Our presence is requested—no, demanded—at headquarters."

Sam glanced at his wrist again. "That's not a royal we. Mrs. Salters is insistent that I bring you along."

Chapter 28

They'd added a whiteboard to the wall of the dining room at the Formby house, and scrawled a series of dates and events on it in various colors. Left alone in the room, Jake studied the information. He didn't recognize the ones at the top of the list, but at the bottom were the most recent, including everything that had happened locally. No matter how he tried, he couldn't connect the dots.

On the right side, Thomason's name had been scribbled in red marker. Jake had been betrayed more than once, but this cut him deep. Not that he ever expected to be friends with Thomason, but Jake thought he knew how to read people, and the cop had never seemed the type to be involved in anything illegal. How much of Jake's reputation in Oak Grove had been created by Thomason playing the long con? After all, he'd been responsible for Jake's original arrest.

"That's a development I never expected," Salters said, coming into the room carrying two beers in glass bottles. She handed one to Jake. "I think I owe you."

Barehanded, he yanked off the metal lid, and noticed the callouses weren't as thick as they used to be. Too many days without working had softened them. He took a deep swig. It was a quality brew, but the flavor wasn't as important at the moment as the alcohol content. "I still don't believe it."

"It explains a lot. The attacks on you, the bogus information leaked about a potential threat on Harmony, the warring office politics among the police force."

Jake froze. *After all this?* "Are you saying Harmony isn't in danger?"

"The new translation makes it appear that way. Now, I don't think Thomason influenced that, but he could have used it to his advantage. Got everyone so focused on her, he could do what he wanted with no questions."

"What does the chatter on the police secure band say?"

"We haven't shared the info with the locals yet. And we still don't have access to their private communications."

Jake chugged down a quarter of the bottle. "Do you have the equipment to hack in?"

Salters grinned. "Yes, but I'm not allowed to tell you that."

"I have a theory. A few nights ago, Thomason brought a debugger from the cop shop to check Harmony's house for listening devices. That's the night we found a tag in my cast."

It was his turn to grin. "You didn't know about that, did you? Anyway, I watched over his shoulder when he entered the password for the machine. What if they've reused the same number to make it easier to remember?"

"One thing at a time. What happened to your cast?"

"There was a fill-in tech at the clinic the day I had it replaced. I figured Houck was involved. Thomason said he'd check it out."

"And then he disappeared."

"Yes."

Salters closed her eyes and rubbed her temples. "Un-freaking-believable. I don't even know how to add that to the scoreboard."

Jake picked up a whiteboard marker. "7-4-2-9" he wrote. Then he emptied his beer. "You didn't hear it from me."

"And I can testify to that in court." She used the eraser to get rid of traces of the number. "I'll let you know how it goes in a few minutes."

She left behind her unopened bottle, tempting Jake. But he suddenly yearned for her approval and grabbed water from the sideboard instead. He drank it as he paced the room, stopping each round to stare at the whiteboard. There had to be another explanation.

He took a moment to retrieve his watch and phone before Salters returned.

"It worked," she said, with no note of celebration in her voice. "There's already been mention of Thomason having abandoned his duty station."

"I'm grasping at straws here, but what if he's undercover? Not for Oak Grove? Something outside his jurisdiction?" Jake asked.

"If it was for a federal agency, I'd know. That leaves the state level, and they are working with us."

"How about the county? The sheriff's department? Chief Santos would have to approve the assignment, and he's been trying to force Thomason into retirement. Maybe this is his way of doing it?"

"Either that or to get him killed." Salters' jaw clenched. "It would explain a lot. Except where is his wife? We're monitoring their bank accounts and neither has spent any money."

"She's a hostage, and he's working with the crooks until he can free her?"

Salters shook her head. "That sounds like a cheap movie plot. Or something out of those drugstore romance books Harmony reads when no one is looking."

"Does she have any theories?" He'd been avoiding her, not knowing what secrets she was keeping from him, and worried about the ones he was keeping from her.

Silence was Jake's answer. He swiveled to face Salters. "You haven't told her."

"And she hasn't asked. Granted, that may be because I've been keeping her busy with analyzing documents during the day and reminiscing at night, but still… By the way, she hasn't asked about you, either."

That stung. Which was what Salters wanted. "She probably figures you chased me away."

"That's what my gut tells me to do. Instead, I'm asking for a favor."

"The beer was a bribe? Or just softening me up so I'm more likely to say yes?"

"Neither. I meant it as a thank you for the assistance you've given. I didn't know I was going to need more."

Jake crossed his arms. "What do you want from me?"

Salters pulled a chair away from the table and sat. With a sweep of her hand, she indicated Jake should do the same.

Once he was seated, she continued. "With the evidence Agent Matney gathered, I am confident in requesting a search warrant at the federal level. Bypass the local judges. Trouble is, he can't remember the address or how to get there. We tried to retrieve the information from his electronics, but the signal was too spotty to be definitive."

"In Sam's defense, he was busy sightseeing."

"And enjoying some much-needed downtime. I won't fault him for it. Will you take him back?"

"You're only going to get one shot. There's not enough traffic to hide additional trips. If we go to verify the address, it'll be suspicious and may blow the entire operation."

"You can locate it on our mapping program." Salters aimed her watch at the screen and brought up the menu. "The controls are intuitive if you want to grab the keyboard."

It took Jake longer to get adjusted to the feel of the built-in mouse than the program. As he narrowed in on the area outside of town, Sam and two other agents joined them. Jake acknowledged their presence with a nod.

He highlighted one large house surrounded by outbuildings and green fields, the images having been captured during the summer. "This is the place I wanted to show you, Sam. The same family has owned and worked it as far back as the records go."

Using it as a starting point, Jake followed a cobweb of roads to get to the second location. "This is where we spotted the cars."

"Snag that address for me," Salters said. "Let's get the warrants rolling. Hennessey, will you zoom in? I want to scan for evidence of illegal activities when this was taken."

Jake did as she asked, then handed the controls over to Sam. This was a job for the experts.

❀ ❀ ❀

Jake had witnessed an FBI raid once, when the clubhouse of a biker gang suspected of human trafficking had been targeted, but he wasn't anticipating the somber mood of the agents as they prepared for this one. There'd been plenty of discussion earlier, as they debated tactics and approaches while waiting for the warrants. The mix of agencies had complicated the issue, each wanting to deploy their favored technique. Now, they were nearly silent as they loaded their gear and strapped on artillery and bullet-proof vests.

He could have walked out the door, but didn't have anywhere he wanted to go. Besides, he felt an unexpected loyalty to this group. He'd lived his life thumbing his nose at the establishment and rooting for the underdog, and he didn't understand what had changed. Maybe it was his devotion to Harmony or Thomason's betrayal—he wasn't sure, but a psychologist would get rich unraveling the knots.

Salters and one agent were staying behind to keep communications flowing. Harmony's current bodyguard would stay in place as well, but the group was meeting an attachment of State Police nearer to the house. There were no reliable figures for how many people were at the location, so the plans assumed a worst case scenario. Sam would make the decisions on-site. Another reminder of Sam's expertise, and how Salters had tried to manipulate Jake.

With the lights in the kitchen turned off, the first four agents headed out the door into the darkness of the backyard to their vehicle. That left three ready for action, including Sam. Jake sat at a desk, staying out of the way and watching Sam and Salters having a whispered conference. They had their backs to him, so he couldn't read their lips.

Sam picked up a bullet-proof vest from the table in the dining room. He already wore one. Had Salters changed her mind and decided to go?

"Coming, Hennessey?" he asked.

It took every bit of Jake's many years of experience to not allow the excitement he felt to reach his face. He did arch his eyebrows in a genuine expression of surprise. "Excuse me?"

"You can identify Thomason and perhaps other locals. Tell us who we are dealing with." Sam glanced at Salters. "This goes against every procedure that's ever been written, but you've never been one to follow the rules. You'll stay in the car until we secure the premises, and of course, you won't be given a weapon."

"I wouldn't take it, anyway. But I have a request. I've

always wanted to test a vehicle spec'd out like the FBI's. Let me drive?"

Jake wasn't allowed to drive. But when they stopped half a mile away, lights off, waiting for everyone to get into place, Sam had more instructions for him.

"We're going to park at the end of the driveway," he said, his voice tight. "I'll leave the car running, but the doors should be locked. You'll take over the driver's seat and position the vehicle for a quick exit. It frees up an agent for the initial entry."

As if that would be enough to satisfy me. "I can do that, but let's hope it isn't needed."

"From your mouth…" Sam muttered. His watch dinged, and a message flashed on his sleeve. "And we have liftoff."

The revolver that Sam had pulled out of his waistband and laid on the console taunted Jake. He had no intention of touching it, but it seemed like a validation of sorts, a symbol of the trust they'd developed. Or was it a trap? He'd lived too long on the wrong side of society to take anything at face value.

Using the rear camera and the car's mirrors, Jake kept an eye on the house. It had been in near-total darkness when they arrived. When the initial confusion caused by flash bangs and the simultaneous breaking down of three doors was over, the action had moved inside and there wasn't much to see, even though everything was lit up like a Christmas tree. With the car windows down, the yelling and occasional gunshots told him the raid was not going smoothly. But he'd heard no calls for medical assistance, either.

A shadow moved where no shadow belonged. Jake had been that shadow too many times to count. He almost wished the shadow well—almost—but he was playing for a different team this time. So, he tracked the figure as it moved towards the cars.

Jake lost sight of the man when he slipped between two of the vehicles. No car came to life with its engine purring or lights adding to the already-bright yard. A car couldn't get past him in the driveway, anyway. The text message he sent to Sam said as much.

Then, a second shadow caught his attention. This one wasn't nearly as cautious as the first. He ran boldly from the house to the cars. Jake sent another, more urgent text and hoped Sam would have time to read it.

And there it was—the signal Jake had waited for. The brief flare of headlights before they were extinguished. They were about to make a break for it, but there was nowhere for them to go.

Sam dashed out of the front door, his head swiveling as he searched for the men and the car. Warren was close behind him. Jake couldn't pick out the right vehicle among the many parked in the yard.

Jake steeled himself for the possibility that they would attempt to ram the agents' car out of the way, but didn't think they could work up enough speed to make it happen. To be on the safe side, he double-checked that the auxiliary braking system was engaged.

At the same time, he plotted his strategy for interfering if the fugitive's car was turned into a weapon to be used against the Feds.

But the two men had a different plan. The car's tires spun in the dirt, found a grip, and they were on their way, bouncing madly towards the open field. Sam and Warren chased after them, but the uneven ground slowed their efforts.

Jake remembered the tractor path at the edge of the field he'd spotted when they'd spied on the house earlier. If the fleeing car made it that far, they had a chance of joining the dirt road and then the paved county lane.

He unlocked the doors, beeped the horn to get Sam's attention, and put the car into low gear. He'd have to use every trick in the book and create a few new ones to make this work. Thankfully, Sam and Warren understood what Jake wanted and headed in his direction. Their doors weren't even fully closed before Jake took off.

"This car isn't built for cross-country," Sam said as he fastened his seatbelt.

"I figured as much. Theirs isn't either. They'll join the road soon." Jake hoped his theory was right.

"They have a head start. Will you be able to catch them?" Warren asked from the back seat.

"I won't know until I try." He shifted into high.

Warren grunted as they flew over a pothole Jake didn't avoid, and one wheel landed hard. This was pure speed and no technique. All Jake was worried about was keeping control of the car.

"There they are," Sam said, leaning forward. "Faster."

Jake clenched the steering wheel. "I'm going as fast

as the car will handle. Any chance of getting roadblocks set up?"

"We maxed out available manpower on the raid."

"The county lane isn't far. If it were me, I'd turn left, which puts me on a road that intersects with a second that leads to the interstate. I have the impression our vehicles are about equal. I can follow and you can pray they make a mistake, or we can trust my gut and do the unexpected."

"What's that?"

Jake barely tapped the manual brakes and swung hard to the left.

"There's no road here," Warren protested.

"Nope." Jake sped up as his tires met concrete. "But a couple of years ago, the county spent a bunch of money building a bike path around the county line. It was supposed to attract tourists, but the money ran out before the path was finished."

Bare branches scraped against the sides of the car. "It's wide enough for a vehicle, and will meet the road in a few miles. It should put us in front of them."

"You've done this before?" Sam asked.

"Rumor says it's been done—but not by me. Hang on to your hats, gents."

Chapter 29

This section of the bike trail was about two miles long, but it cut five miles off the trip on the back country roads. Jake had anticipated the broken pavement and narrow spots. The bridge over the small creek worried him, but the car fit—barely. The deer that bolted across the trail surprised him, but he held the vehicle to the path as he applied the brakes. He hadn't accounted for broken branches, but they were small enough that he ran over them. The undercarriage of the car would never be the same, but the Feds had deep pockets.

They were doing forty when they hit the paved road, pulling in behind a semi. It would serve as camouflage until they determined their status.

"See anyone behind us?" he asked, checking his mirrors.

"You sure they aren't in front of us?" Warren asked, twisting around.

"I was watching for headlights as we neared the road. Didn't spot anyone else. They could be a couple of miles back."

"If they are, I can't see them." Warren turned to face forward again. "That was one wild ride."

"It's the most fun I've had in months. Are you able to identify the occupants of the car if we stop it? I didn't see faces."

"That's my job. I put trackers on all the vehicles before the raid. The search warrant covers the procedure. The tags are in a spot where they need to get the car up on a lift to find them."

So, Warren was more than he seemed, too. Jake slowed, wanting to give the suspect's car time to catch up. "Remind me to have my car checked out when you guys leave town. I assume your watch can locate your tag?"

"Within range, yes."

"Then see if you can pick up something now. There's a car hanging a hill or so back, but I'm spotting its headlights every so often."

Warren fiddled with the device on his wrist. "Nothing. Either it's too far away or you guessed wrong."

Jake didn't want to believe it. "Or the hills are blocking the signal. I'll slow down more and see if that helps."

The headlights in the sky seemed brighter this time as the other car topped a small ridge.

"Got it," Warren reported. "We're in business."

"Do you want them stopped? Or to play cat and mouse until you can bring in additional units? We're close to the interstate, and the possibility of high speeds and civilian traffic."

"You're thinking like a cop, Hennessey," Sam said.

"Too much time spent watching crime shows. I can

force a stop, but I won't guarantee this car will be drivable afterwards. Your call. You have two miles to decide."

"Do it," Sam and Warren said at the same time.

Jake longed for the days when he could pull off a Bootlegger's 180—it would be fun to show off for the Feds. He'd tried with these newer cars, but had no luck. No manual clutch, no fine control of speed and brakes, even the steering wasn't as responsive.

He settled for using a combination of the system brake and the manual emergency break, along with pushing the steering as far as it would go to end up sideways on the road, the nose of the car well into the other lane. The wet pavement allowed the tires to achieve an extra few inches of the spin. Not Jake's prettiest work, but he'd take it. He completed the turn in a more traditional fashion, then proceeded as fast as the car would let him go.

"We've got to get the Academy to add that maneuver," Sam said as he let go of the grasp he'd had on the dash. "What else do you have in your bag of tricks?"

Headlights popped up over a small hill. "Is that our target?" Jake asked.

"Yes." Warren confirmed.

Jake swerved into the other lane, going the wrong way. "Anyone up for a game of chicken?"

The driver of the other car wasn't. Ready to play chicken, that was. When Jake chose a path down the middle of the road, going full speed and flashing his lights, there was nowhere for the driver to go but into the ditch. He took the safe way out and came to a full stop on the pavement. Then he and his passenger bailed out of their vehicle and made a run for it. Jake braked so the agency car's bumper touched theirs.

Sam and Warren were prepared. Before Jake had brought the car to a full stop, they jumped out, guns in hands.

"FBI. On the ground, NOW!" Sam shouted.

A shot pinged off the agency car, and Jake ducked, glad he was wearing the bullet-proof vest. Not that it would help if he was hit in the head. He was tempted to pick up the revolver Sam had left, but he'd be a liability in a gun battle, not an asset. The two men fled, and Sam and Warren were already in pursuit. Jake forced the headlights to high beam to provide better lighting.

In a few minutes, a helicopter hovered overhead, shining spotlights on the fields below. Then a sheriff's car with a police dog showed up. Jake figured it was all but over, but the cleanup would take forever. He hoped someone would give him a ride back to town.

"We've got another favor to ask," Sam said, taking off his vest and leaning against the agency car.

Jake had taken off his sometime ago, despite the sudden drop in temperature, and was pacing near the car to stay alert. "Is that the royal we this time?"

"Yes, and no. I've received Mrs. Salters' permission to ask you, but it's my idea."

"This can't be good." Jake closed his eyes and rubbed his forehead. He was too tired to deal with anything else without a strong cup of coffee—or, better yet, whiskey.

"You know, we're using the county facilities to process everyone we took into custody tonight."

"The bust was in their jurisdiction."

Sam nodded. "The suspects understood their rights. They've all asked for a lawyer, which won't happen until business hours. That's still several hours away."

"Smart of them."

"Yes. Thomason was among the people arrested."

"Fuck." Jake dropped his head and stared at the small rocks at the edge of the road. "I was hoping I was wrong."

"He wants to talk with you."

Jake's head jerked back up. "What?"

The agent quirked his mouth. "He says he has important information you need to know. He's afraid it will get lost if he doesn't tell you directly."

"What's he playing at?"

"We aren't sure. But we won't allow you to be alone with him, and he's agreed to you being accompanied by one LEO of your choosing."

"A few days ago, that would have been him."

"Yeah."

Jake studied Sam's face. "I'm guessing you want to be the one with me."

Sam grinned. "I've been outranked. Mrs. Salters formally requests that she be the one in the room with you. You can decline the request—both of them—but it would really help us out if you do it."

❋ ❋ ❋

It wasn't right, seeing Thomason in cuffs. And Jake

suspected there were shackles securing the detective's ankles as well. The old jeans and sweatshirt the detective wore had seen better days, with tears that looked new. There'd be developing bruises under those clothes if Jake had to make a guess. He dipped his chin in greeting. "Thomason."

"Jake. And the lady is?"

"Vanessa Salters, DHS. She and I collaborated on a case involving Harmony years ago, and they've remained friends. Do you need more credentials than that?"

Thomason shook his head. "That's good enough for me. This is off the record, and there are no recordings being made, correct?"

"That's why we're in an office instead of an interview room," Salters pointed out.

Thomason leaned forward and focused on Jake. "You're still in danger."

"Explain," Salters demanded.

Thomason's eyes remained glued to Jake's. "Remember the group in the neighborhood where you were attacked? The ones tied to the threats against Harmony? It's you they are after. They have this weird idea that you're responsible for spiriting away one of the young women who wasn't happy with the marriage they'd arranged for her."

It took every ounce of control for Jake to keep his expression blank. "I've been accused of crazier things, but not by much."

"Where did you get the information, Thomason?" Salters asked.

"I can't reveal my source yet. Let's just say other

members of the group are unhappy with the lifestyle."

"I'm going to go out on a limb and guess they're also tied to the counterfeiting ring. What are their names?"

"The only way I can assure their safety is to make sure they're treated like everyone else. I'm not convinced there isn't a leak in the department, although I haven't identified it."

"I can put them into federal protection."

"That could take months," Thomason protested. "From the little I know, an office in Washington handles that. Do you have those connections?"

Salters smiled. "Hennessey didn't mention my title. Deputy Assistant Director. I *am* the office you need."

"Is Chief Santos aware you're doing this?" Jake asked as he stood and started wandering around the room. He stopped to study the paperwork on a bulletin board, pulling down one multi-paged set.

"When the opportunity arose to infiltrate the group, I had to take it. I called him, but was sent to his voice mail. No surprise, he's been ignoring me." Thomason shrugged. "I don't know if he bothered to listen to the message. I've been out of touch. It makes my cover story more believable—that I'm upset that Santos got the chief position instead of me, and this is my revenge."

"What are you doing, Hennessey?" Salters asked.

"Looking for a paperclip or something. I need to get Thomason out of those cuffs. He doesn't deserve to be in them." Jake abandoned the bulletin board and tried opening a nearby file cabinet, but it was locked as well. "I can't believe you were stupid enough to risk your career and your life for me, Thomason. Especially this close to retirement."

"And now you are setting yourself up to spend the rest of your life in prison just to free him?" Salters asked.

Jake stopped in his tracks. "Yeah, I guess I am."

"Damn do-gooders." Salters shook her head. "Restoring my faith in humanity and all that. And you, Hennessey, you're supposed to be the bad guy, not the knight in shining armor."

"Sorry to disappoint you."

"I didn't do it for you, Hennessey," Thomason said quietly. "I did it for Harmony."

And there it is. It always led back to Harmony. Jake would never have her to himself. Too many other people loved her, too.

"Except you missed the updates the last few days. Turns out Harmony wasn't in danger. The information was mistranslated." Salters rubbed her neck. "Loosely paraphrased, it said she wasn't a threat anymore because the U.S. government no longer trusted her."

"So, this whole thing was a sham?"

"The cast on Hennessey's arm and the federal agent in the hospital say otherwise."

Thomason's forehead wrinkled. "Who got hurt?"

"Special Agent Houck. He's in recovery, but I don't have time to explain the entire story. There's work to be done. Starting with getting you back to headquarters for a debriefing. And you telling us how to contact your wife to tell her you're safe."

The furrows in Thomason's forehead deepened. "You don't know? She's with Harmony."

Salters groaned. "Of course she is. I wondered why Harmony was suddenly hungry all the time. I thought it was the change in meds."

She turned to Jake. "Have you found something to get the cuffs off Thomason or am I going to have to fight the sheriff? I'm not in the mood for it."

Jake had been working at a rough spot on the back of his waistband. He pulled out a short metal wire, then turned to Salters. "You won't see this, right?"

"See what?"

In homage to the sacrifice Thomason had made, Jake knelt to start at the ankles. The shackles were basic, and it took Jake mere seconds to unlock them. He stood and stretched as they clanked on the floor.

"Just like that," Salters said.

"Cheap models," Jake explained. "Even Sam would be able to unlock them. The wrist ones look newer and should be more of a challenge."

"I won't tell Agent Matney you said that," she grinned.

"Who are you talking about?" Thomason asked, as Jake held his wrists.

"The FBI agent Hennessey has been paired with."

Thomason's mouth dropped open as the cuff from his right wrist fell into his lap. Jake switched his attention to the left one.

"I'm going to have to go back and review your files, Hennessey," Salters said.

The second cuff opened. "Don't waste your time. You won't find what you're looking for," Jake told her.

"I can't use it against you, anyway."

"Nope. That's what happens when you make a deal with the devil."

"I'll keep that in mind. For now, let's concentrate on getting Detective Thomason out of here with a minimum of fuss."

Chapter 30

Jake wanted to steal away to his crummy little apartment and get drunk. Instead, he was sequestered in the room on the third floor of Harmony's house, with nothing to comfort him but a cold cup of coffee and a warm bottle of water. The many loud conversations happening downstairs drifted up the stairwell and kept him awake.

Harmony was worried that he remained in danger. Salters wanted him around for legal purposes. Chief Santos was searching for a way to arrest him for obstruction of justice or auto theft or some other bullshit, because Jake hadn't revealed the location of Thomason's car.

Thomason and Sarah were in a room on the second floor, spending quality time together. Thomason had wanted to go home, but Salters had overruled his request until her team completed clean-up work. The original setup had been Harmony's idea—inspired, she said, by a TV show. Jake knew better. She'd been on the phone with Sarah and overheard Thomason's plans to infiltrate the counterfeiters, and insisted Sarah would be safer staying with her. It turned out that Sarah had refilled her prescriptions a few days before going into hiding and had taken the new bottles with her.

Jake amused himself by plotting a path to get away without being spotted. From the small third-floor room at the back of the house, he could crawl out the window and drop to the ground. It would be a long fall with no cushioning and not worth the risk. Besides, two deputy marshals patrolled outside, and earlier in the afternoon, a winter storm had moved in, dropping copious amounts of snow. No, he'd remain where he was.

But he couldn't hide away forever. After all the law enforcement left, he'd still have to deal with Harmony.

Jake's watch beeped repeatedly, waking him up from a light snooze. Two messages waited for him, one from Harmony saying food had been delivered, the other from his security system. Someone had broken into his apartment, and his camera wasn't responding.

He shoved his feet into his shoes, grabbed his keys, and flew down the steps, taking them two at a time. Ignoring everyone else, he stopped in front of Salters, who sat in the living room with a filled plate. "Why?"

She put her food on the end table. "Why what?"

"Why do you have someone in my apartment?"

"I don't." She grabbed her phone and stood.

Jake didn't wait to see what she was up to. He dashed out the front door. His car was a block away, and he made it there in record time, but not fast enough to shake Sam, who'd followed him, his bullet-proof vest in his hands. Jake didn't waste his breath fighting the agent's presence and unlocked the car.

"Talk to me," Sam said as they fastened their seatbelts.

"Hold on." Jake squealed the tires as he pulled into the street. He punched a button on the console. "Call Lonnie."

The phone connected and rang. And rang. And rang until it switched to voice mail. The windshield wipers squeaked as they swiped back and forth, keeping the glass mostly clean.

"Shit." Jake disconnected.

"Who's Lonnie?" Sam asked.

"My landlord. He could be asleep, have the TV turned up too loud, or be passed out drunk."

"Or he could be in trouble with whoever broke into your apartment."

"Right."

While Sam passed the information to Salters, Jake concentrated on avoiding traffic and getting to his apartment, running red lights and breaking the speed limit.

"Mrs. Salters is sending several agents as backup," Sam said. "I hope it's a false alarm and we won't need them."

"Don't count on it." Jake turned right without braking or signaling. The move threw Sam against the door, despite his seatbelt. "We're almost there."

"What makes this different from when we searched your apartment a few days ago?"

"It was clear you were the Feds the minute you walked

in, and I expected it. Tonight, the cameras are disabled, and I suspect they've turned off the electricity. Not law enforcement's normal way of operating."

"True. Any weapons we need to worry about?"

"A few kitchen knives. A frying pan. How many times do I have to tell you I don't do guns?" Jake turned into the alley that led to his back door. He dimmed the car's headlights before creeping closer.

"What's the plan?" Sam asked.

"I don't have one. Just follow my lead." After parking behind the neighbor's house, Jake scanned the area. Falling snow glittered in the rays of lightfrom the other houses. Only Lonnie's was dark.

The first thing he noted when he got out of the car was that Bob, Lonnie's dog, wasn't on the back porch. Sure, Lonnie might have brought him inside because of the snow, but Bob liked the cold weather. Getting closer, he saw a trail of footprints leading towards the house and the rake and bucket of water had been moved. He watched his windows for any stray beam of light sneaking through the curtains, but there was none.

He retreated to the back gate. Sam followed him, slipping on his vest as they walked. "It feels like a trap," Jake explained in a whisper.

"Do you want to wait for assistance?"

It was tempting. Let the experts handle it. But damn it, this was his humble home and Lonnie was a friend. "No. I'm going in. Just giving you fair warning, I don't know what I'm walking into. You can come or not."

"I've got your back."

Jake nodded. "Let's do it."

He sprinted towards the house. Not trying to be quiet, he hit the stairs at full speed, didn't stop when he reached the landing, then rammed the door with his shoulder. It flew open. Not giving his eyes time to adjust, he dove to the floor behind the beat-up sofa.

He peeked around the corner of the couch and spotted… no one and nothing. Enough light filtered in from the neighbors to allow Jake to see an untouched room.

Gun outstretched, Sam rushed through the door. Jake stood and shrugged, then put his finger to his lips. He jerked his head towards the bedroom. Sam nodded.

Jake had memorized every loose board under the tattered carpet and moved across the room without stepping on even one. Sam didn't have that advantage. If anyone was in the bedroom, they'd hear him coming.

But Jake got there first. Although Sam was the one with the gun, this was Jake's home and his responsibility. He peered around the door frame to find another empty room. From the bed with its covers halfway on the floor to the open closet, everything was how he'd left it. Even the cardboard boxes he kept in a pile in front of the fake wall in the closet were where they belonged. That left the tiny bathroom. Sam shouldered Jake out of the way and pushed the door open with his foot.

Empty.

Sam lowered his arms. "Did your landlord forget to pay the electric bill?"

"They only do shutoffs during business hours." Jake

strode back to the other room to examine the front door.
"Sam. Look."

"What?"

"It's cracked open. The door catches on the wood
frame sometimes. I have to give it an extra jerk to close
it correctly."

"Anyone else live here? Besides your landlord?"

"No. There's an empty room down the hall."

"Try calling him. See if we can hear his phone
ringing."

Downstairs, a dog barked and then yelped. "If they
hurt Bob . . ." Jake clenched his fists.

"Bob?"

"Lonnie's dog." Jake was already on his way out the
back door. "Nobody hurts Bob when I'm around."

"Where are you going?"

Jake stopped long enough for Sam to catch up. "The
basement. Whoever is in there will expect me to come in
the front door or down the interior steps. But another set
comes up from the cellar to the kitchen. I can stage an
attack from the rear."

"Any way to check out the situation in Lonnie's part
of the house?"

"Without being seen? No."

"Then we'll split up. You take the basement. I'll run a
distraction out front."

It was an option Jake hadn't considered. He was used
to working alone. He nodded. "I'll ping you when I'm in
place. Good hunting."

Sam cocked his head. "What?"

"I've heard it used by some semi-regular customers. I

see them a couple of times a year. It seemed appropriate."

"I like it. Good hunting, Hennessey."

Jake had often helped Lonnie with repairs in the basement, but it was a jumble of tools and broken furniture, so he used his phone's flashlight to navigate the path between the window he'd crawled through and the stairway. He didn't have the creaky spots of these stairs mapped in his brain, so he stayed close to the edge of the steps. His approach wasn't as silent as he'd hoped.

On the top step, he sent a quick text to Sam. "*Here.*" Without waiting for a response, he tested the doorknob. Unlocked, as he had expected. The doorbell rang, and Jake used the moment to open the basement door.

There were no footsteps headed toward the front entrance. Not a good sign. Sam's distraction hadn't worked. Jake took the last step and slid into the kitchen.

From somewhere in the house, he caught Bob's soft whining. At least the dog was still alive. The front doorknob rattled, and Jake assumed it was Sam, trying to get in. He considered dashing across the hallway to open it, but that left him exposed. He hoped Sam had a paperclip and that he'd get in before Jake died.

He glanced around the kitchen, looking for a weapon, but Lonnie had fewer utensils than he did. The old man lived off takeout and microwaved dinners.

The doorbell rang again. Nothing changed.

Jake stuck his head around the corner to check out the living room, then withdrew. In the little light provided by the streetlights through the flimsy curtains, he'd spotted Lonnie in his worn-out easy chair, seemingly asleep. No different from any other evening. But the silhouette behind him holding a gun didn't belong there.

"It took you long enough to show up, Hennessey," a man's voice said. "You might as well show yourself."

The outside doorknob rattled again. If Jake delayed long enough, Sam might figure it out. "Who are you?" he asked.

"It doesn't matter. Toss any weapons you have on the floor and show yourself."

"Or else?"

"It might be fun to start with the dog."

Bob yelped and whimpered, and Jake assumed he'd been kicked. He couldn't allow that to happen again. Hands spread out at his sides, he turned the corner between the kitchen and the living room. "Here I am. What do you want?"

"To kill you. But first you have to tell me where she is."

"Where who is?" Jake asked.

"Toss me your weapons," the man demanded.

Jake raised his outstretched hands and studied the man's face in the limited light. He didn't look familiar. "I don't carry. Everyone knows that."

"Right. Like I believe that story. You run the shadiest bar around and you don't have a gun?"

"Not even a taser. Come, search me." If Jake got the man closer, he might be able to take him down with a few well-placed punches. His cast made an excellent weapon.

The man came out from behind Lonnie's chair, but stayed several yards away. "Where is she?"

"I don't know who you are talking about."

"Sure you do. Marissa Pearson. She disappeared six months ago. You're responsible. I hoped you'd run and lead us to her, but it didn't work. So, now you're dead."

That wasn't a name Jake remembered. "I don't know her."

"How could you forget her? She was perfect, and her parents promised her to me."

"What makes you think I had anything to do with it?"

"Everyone knows you run a human trafficking ring."

Jake blinked. Of all the things that might have come out of the man's mouth, that was the last thing he'd expected.

The front door crashed open. "FBI," Sam yelled. "Drop your weapon."

The man twisted, his revolver aimed at Sam. Jake had one chance. He threw himself across the room. The shot was fired before Jake hit his target.

Chapter 31

Jake and Sam sat on the interior stairs, staying out of the way, while the EMTs carried Lonnie out of the house on a stretcher. They believed he'd been overdosed with his pain medication, and he was being airlifted to a hospital in Pittsburgh for observation. They'd checked out Sam, but his bulletproof vest had done its job. He'd have a bruise on his chest, but nothing more.

The attacker hadn't fared so well. Jake had not only pummeled him with his good fist, he'd used his cast like a baton to beat him. The cast had cracked, and the EMTs had wrapped it in an elastic bandage until Jake could get in to see Doc Gabe.

"I never suspected we'd be busting a corrupt cop," Sam said as several of the U.S. Marshals hauled Morrison out of the house. "I figured we were just dealing with a cult."

"You got both. A cop that was a member of a cult. Morrison's arrest won't go down well with the City Council, and Chief Santos will have lots of explaining to do. That and figuring out who was friends with

Morrison and keeping his eye on them. I don't think he's up to the task and we'll see a new chief in a few years." Jake rubbed his left wrist where the cast had scraped his skin during the fight.

"Thomason?"

"Nope. He turned down the job once. I don't see him wanting to tackle it now."

"Where did Morrison get the idea that you were involved in human trafficking?"

"My guess is that the rumor mill picked up whispers of another activity I've been involved in, and it mutated."

"I'll ask Salters to scrub any mention of that hobby from the official records."

Jake stared outside, where the ambulance was pulling away. "I've become a security risk. Well, I was already a risk, but in a different way. I'll need to find a new way to support the cause."

"You really didn't have anything to do with the young woman that Morrison was looking for?"

"Honestly, it wasn't me, but I would have helped her if I'd known about her. A sixteen-year-old girl is still a kid, and Morrison is what, thirty?"

"I dealt with a group like this once. They claimed if a girl wasn't married by the time she was sixteen, it was a disgrace." Sam rubbed his chest where the bullet had hit.

"I hope that however Marissa got out, she sets an example for other girls."

"Chances are they will migrate back to Tennessee now that they've been tied to the counterfeiting case."

Tennessee? Not Sweden? Jake filed away the information

to ponder later. "What's the deal with that, anyway? How'd I get mixed in with that?"

"Another way to destroy your reputation? If he could manufacture enough evidence to tie you to their operations, you'd be an easy scapegoat and protect them."

"No matter how hard I try, I'll always be the bad guy."

They watched as Morrison was forced into the back seat of an agency car. Salters was having an animated discussion with Chief Santos over jurisdiction. Jake couldn't figure out why the chief was even trying. The case was way out of his league.

"So, what is your plan for the rest of the night?" Sam asked as the agency car pulled away, headed for Pittsburgh. Or Cleveland. There'd been a debate on which office to use, and Jake hadn't overheard the final decision. Something about isolating him from the other detainees.

"There's no chance of getting any sleep here tonight, so I'll grab a bottle from my stash and head over to the hotel. If I hurry, I might be in time to pick up some food from the Dairy Barn before they close." And now that he knew the right channel, he'd listen in on Oak Grove's secure police band until he fell asleep.

"Sounds like a plan. Better than the late night I'll put in doing paperwork." Sam nodded towards the street, where the discussion between Salters and Santos had finished. "But if I were you, I'd take off before Mrs. Salters gets it in her head that she needs you to answer more questions."

The first glass of whiskey went down smooth. Too smooth. Jake was going to have to watch himself if he didn't want to get drunk without reaching the mellow stage first.

With his award-winning smile, and a heavy dose of flirting, he'd talked Mary, his favorite waitress, into coercing the cook to make one last order before shutting down the grill. Nothing complicated—just a grilled cheese sandwich and a bowl of their chicken noodle soup. He'd also remembered to buy a bag of pretzels for Anton at the hotel's front desk.

He wasn't alone, technically. An unmarked Oak Grove police vehicle had followed him from his apartment. Either the officer wanted to be seen or needed lessons in stealth. Jake suspected there was an agency car behind him, but at least they knew what they were doing. Both had parked in the hotel parking lot near Jake's car.

Jake ate his sandwich before it got cold. The soup, he saved for later. He wanted to establish his presence in his "official" room before moving to the second one. He'd set his phone and watch to "do not disturb" so the cops could still track him, but he'd have time to himself.

So, he only half expected the knock on his door. As he gulped down the remains of his second whiskey, he made a mental bet about who it was. Sam? Not likely. Salters? A possibility, but not probable. Thomason? Unlikely. He settled on a random Oak Grove cop doing Santos' bidding to bring him in for questioning on a dubious charge.

He lost the bet. At the next knock, he looked out

the peephole. An angel stood there, with a glowering guardian behind her.

Jake opened the door. "Hello, Angel, Warren."

Once Warren had checked out the shabby room, he left Harmony and Jake alone, taking a protective stance leaning against the wall in the hallway.

"Care for a drink, Angel?" Jake asked as he closed the door.

She settled herself on the lone chair, resting her cane against the bed. "How many have you had?"

"One. I'm pacing myself." He pulled off the lie with a stoic face.

"I almost believe you. But I won't yell at you because you've had a rough night."

"A rough couple of weeks, actually." Jake sat on the bed, whiskey-less. "Why are you here?"

"You've been avoiding me."

"Agreed. I was walking a fine line, and didn't want to involve you. Besides, Salters doesn't like me, and I was staying out of her way."

"I missed you."

Jake reached for the whiskey bottle, poured himself a double shot, and lifted the bottle towards Harmony. She shook her head.

"Are you ready for this discussion, Angel?" he asked, clutching the glass in both hands.

"Probably not. But I realized how quickly I got used to having you around."

"Because I remind you of Eli."

"No. Because you remind me of me. How I used to be. The part of me I lost in the struggle to stay alive. You still see that in me."

"I take it that's a good thing."

"I need to unpack it with my therapist, but yes, it is."

"You still haven't told me why you're here." Jake took a deep sip of his drink.

"We never properly said goodbye. I understand now it wasn't your fault. So, when everything happened, I realized I might never have the chance. And I felt guilty."

His mouth went dry. "You're going back to Florida?"

"No. But if they run you out of town and you go to Cleveland, I might miss my chance."

"I'm not leaving. Oak Grove is my home. Sure, I may take off to Cleveland once you get settled into your new job and while I'm waiting for the bar to be repaired, but I'll be back."

She got up and looked out the window. "They withdrew the job offer."

Jake stood, put his glass on the dresser, and placed his good hand on her shoulder. The touch sent a spark up his arm, and a wave of desire through the rest of his body. He should have known better, but he let his hand stay. "What happened?"

Harmony put her hand on top of his. "The way the grant was written, the library had to pay for my benefits. The Board claims there's no room in the budget for them. Janine is upset, but there's nothing she can do about it."

"Bullshit."

"Yeah, I know. I suspect the real reason is politics.

They thought they were getting a quiet little old lady and got me instead. I'm not the role model they were looking for."

"You're too good for them, Angel. But you'll be fine. You don't need to work."

"Except I've received another offer. The state colleges in the western part of Pennsylvania cooperate. They've offered me a position assisting students, mostly on the master's level, with finding resources for their research. I didn't know a job like that existed."

I wonder who applied pressure to whom to make it happen. At least one person gets their happy ending. "It's the perfect fit."

"Best part is, I can work from wherever I want, even Florida if company business requires my presence."

"The library board has no idea what they are missing."

"Janine suggested I get my revenge by applying for a position on the board. Maybe in a year or two." She patted his hand and let hers drop.

Jake read her body language and stepped back, breaking contact.

She turned to face him. They were still close enough that he could have leaned in and kissed her. He didn't.

"I'm actually looking forward to tomorrow. And the next day. And the day after that," she said. "It's about time. It only took a little danger to wake me up."

"And it turns out you were never in danger at all, except when you were around me. I apologize for that."

Harmony reached out and touched his face. The faint remnants of bruising remained, and she traced them with her finger. "It wasn't your fault. Look how many agencies working together it took to figure it out."

He wanted to take that finger and kiss it. He didn't. "Why are you here, Angel? This could have waited until tomorrow."

"I had to do this while I had the courage." She ran a hand over the top of her head. "I used to love you, Jake."

"And then you met Eli."

She nodded. "And then I met Eli. By the way, Vanessa had the autopsy report of the truck driver who hit us reviewed. It came up with the original answer. He had what she called a 'medical event.' Wouldn't give me the details, but she'd hinted at a cardiac incident. Doan's theory that it was a planned attack is baseless."

Jake had never been able to keep up with the way her mind worked. Sometimes the best option was to wait for her to get to the point. He waited.

"You know Vanessa gave me access to lots of files, letting me feel I was a part of the team, and to keep me busy so I didn't get in the way."

Jake grinned. "I knew you'd figure that out."

"Anyway, she accidentally gave me your full file as well. Not the heavily redacted one she'd shared earlier."

Jake doubted it had been an accident. Salters was too good to make a slip like that.

"It seems the FBI likes to blame cases they can't solve on you, even when they can't make the charges stick. I enjoyed the one where you were accused of stealing a diamond necklace from the mother-in-law at a wedding and it was found a couple of weeks later in a leftover gift bag."

That theft had gone against his normal rules of not

touching anyone in the bridal party, but the mother-in-law had worn a white dress that looked like a bridal gown, and Jake had been determined to ruin her day. Once the necklace was in his hands, he'd realized the stones were fake and of no use to him. He'd ruined her day twice, because when the necklace was located, police experts identified it as nothing but glass and her family and friends found out.

Although he'd abandoned his original target for theft, a matched set of ruby earrings, he'd used the opportunity to lift a sizable amount of cash from the wallet of a guest who was selling drugs. The wait staff received a better-than-average tip before Jake left. All in all, he counted it as a profitable day.

"Don't let that fool you into thinking I'm a good person."

"I'd describe you as a good man with a bad hobby."

"Law enforcement disagrees."

She chuckled. "I've overheard some of their conversations. They have no clue what to believe. At least one wants to write you off as nothing but an urban legend."

"It won't change Salters' opinion of me." *And rightfully so.* "She's a smart lady. You should pay attention to her."

"I should. Instead, I snuck out of the house like a teenager to come see you."

"Which brings us back to the question. Why are you here, Angel?"

"This." She framed his face with her hands and pulled it down to hers.

The temptation proved too much. If this meant

goodbye, he'd pour every bit of his love for her into the moment. He gently wrapped both arms around her and tugged her closer. When she didn't resist, he closed the gap between their mouths and pressed his lips to hers.

Her lips parted and gave him the encouragement he needed. As always, Harmony fought for control as their tongues danced and he allowed her to have it. This was for her, for him, and what they'd once shared. It had to be enough to last him until his memories faded.

She broke away, and he let her go. She stared into his eyes, and after a long moment, nodded. "That's what I thought."

Epilogue

The rubber-tipped cane thunked as it hit the concrete top step, its sound almost drowned out by the noise of hammers and drills in the house across the street. Harmony Duprie-Hennessey stood there, letting herself adjust to the spurt of pain in her left leg. The first stair was always the worst. Jake had suggested building a ramp, but the house wasn't hers anymore. At least, it wouldn't be once it sold. Sarah had pounded an old-fashioned 'For Sale' sign in the yard yesterday.

Jake was in the driveway at the bottom of the stairs, loading her suitcases into the trunk of her car. She appreciated him taking the time to help when he had two major projects in the works, having completed The Purple Onion's renovations last week. He'd jumped on buying the Formby house as soon as it came on the market, and he'd also bought Lonnie's house when Lonnie moved to a retirement home. Jake was still living in his apartment while he fixed up the downstairs in his spare time.

She took a deep breath as she contemplated the short

staircase. It never got better. Well, that wasn't exactly true. Before she bought the house on Ash Street, she'd tested the jetted tub several times, and it had helped for a few minutes. But she'd made Jake work for the sale. He had to install safety bars in the bathroom, bookshelves in both the living room and the master bedroom, and add the spice rack in the kitchen as part of the deal. The masseuse he'd hired to work on her leg weekly wasn't part of the negotiations, but welcomed.

A spring shower wet her face, hiding the tears she couldn't stop. How many more goodbyes would she have to say? At least Jake had invited her to collaborate with him on the Formby house. That should take some of the sting out of selling this one.

Nothing would take away the pain of the trip to Florida. The business part was nothing compared to the planned visit to Eli's grave. She'd avoided it for too long. She'd never be able to move forward until she made her peace with the past.

Jake hadn't offered to go with her, and she hadn't asked. He seemed to understand she needed to do this herself. She took the key out of the pouch on her hip and locked the old-fashioned front door, then turned once again to see him opening the car door for her.

"Ready, Angel?" he asked.

"As ready as I'll ever be."

She limped down the stairs, trying not to wince with each step. He held out the car keys to her. She took them and settled into the front seat, the gull wing door acting as an umbrella. She'd programmed the car for her destination and stops along the way. There was no construction scheduled along the route and once she got south of Pittsburgh, the weather was predicted to be favorable for the entire trip. She closed the car door and rolled down the window.

"Let me know when you get to the hotel tonight," he said, bracing his arm on the roof of the car and leaning down.

The insinuation was clear. He'd take a kiss if she wanted one but wouldn't pressure her for it. She took pity on him and angled her head up, offering what he wished for. It was a quick peck, just a gesture between friends, but it was enough. It wasn't a goodbye, more like a "see you later". They occasionally wandered into something far more, but not this time.

He straightened and patted the roof of the car. She rolled up the window and stroked the dashboard. "Car," she said. She still hadn't named it. "Engage."

THE END

Note to Readers

I didn't expect to write the two Jake Hennessey stories as bookends to the Harmony Duprie Mysteries, but Jake decided you should know his side of the story. Now I can move along to a new project with a clear mind. Paging C.T. McGregor, private investigator. (Yes, I've promised this before. Then Jake intruded.)

A Harmony Duprie Companion Story

The Fall of Jake Hennessey

Jake Hennessey deals in selling fine jewelry of an illegal nature. The thrill of getting away with it is his addiction. When he hears a rumor about a rare old book in the personal collection of a small-town librarian, he gets the urge to try a new game.

After all, even jewel thieves get bored.

But the librarian, Harmony Duprie, isn't what he expected and the challenge becomes serious business.

In order to win, Jake's going to have to play by a new set of rules—and make them up as he goes along—because this time, he's playing for the rest of his life.Books in the

THE CONTESSA'S BROOCH

A firebug is stalking Oak Grove and internet researcher Harmony Duprie is on the case. It starts as a simple data analysis project for Police Chief Sorenson, but things get personal when the house she renovated is targeted.

The arsonist is in it for the glory, posting videos of his exploits on social media. Can Eli, Lando and Scotty, Harmony's favorite computer hackers, help her track down the pyromaniac before someone gets hurt? Or, worse yet, killed?

THE SAMURAI'S INRO

Harmony Duprie has it made. Or so she thinks.
New job.
New routine.
A quiet life in the quiet little town of Oak Grove.
Oh, and Eli.

But trouble has a long memory and it's playing a deadly game.

THE RANGER'S DOG TAGS

It isn't the first time Eli Hennessey has disappeared. Is it the last?

Books in
The Free Wolves Series

WOLVES' PAWN
Book 1

Dot McKenzie is a lone wolf-shifter on the run. Can she survive when she becomes a pawn in a pack leader's deadly game?

WOLVES' KNIGHT
Book 2

Tasha Roeper knows what it means to protect your own. Torn between tradition and a changing world, will Tasha risk everything to save a friend—including her own life—when old enemies arise?

WOLVES' GAMBIT
Book 3

Free Wolf Lori Grenville has made it her life's mission to help unhappy shifters escape from overbearing alphas and dangerous situations. She hasn't failed in a mission yet. This one may be the exception.

P.J. MacLayne
can be reached at:

NEWSLETTER
eepurl.com/cL73Cz

WEBSITE
PJMacLayne.com

FACEBOOK
facebook.com/pjmaclayne

TWITTER
twitter.com/pjmaclayne

BOOKBUB
bookbub.com/profile-p-j-maclyane

AMAZON
amazon.com/P.J.-MacLayne/e/B00HVE8WZI